AUG 3 1 2019

D0538377

Jim Henson's™ FRAGGLE ROCK™

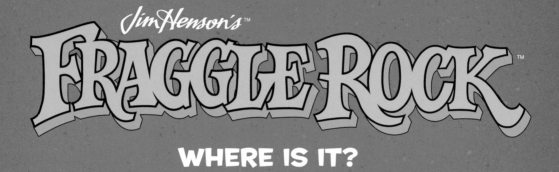

WHERE IS IT?

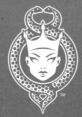

Published by
ARCHAIA™

Series Designer **MICHELLE ANKLEY**
Collection Designer **JILLIAN CRAB**
Assistant Editor **GAVIN GRONENTHAL**
Series Editor **CAMERON CHITTOCK**
Collection Editor **MATTHEW LEVINE**

ARCHAIA™ Jim Henson THE JIM HENSON COMPANY™

BOOM! Studios, 5670 Wilshire Boulevard, Suite 400, Los Angeles, CA 90036-5679. Printed in China. First Printing.

ISBN: 978-1-68415-397-8, eISBN: 978-1-64144-380-7

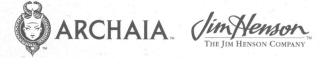

Jim Henson's™ FRAGGLE ROCK™

WHERE IS IT?

by

ART BALTAZAR

Cover Art by
ART BALTAZAR

Special Thanks to
BRIAN HENSON, LISA HENSON, JIM FORMANEK, NICOLE GOLDMAN, CARLA DELLAVEDOVA,
KAREN FALK, BLANCA LISTA, JESSICA MANSOUR, SHANNON ROBLES,
and the entire Jim Henson Company team.

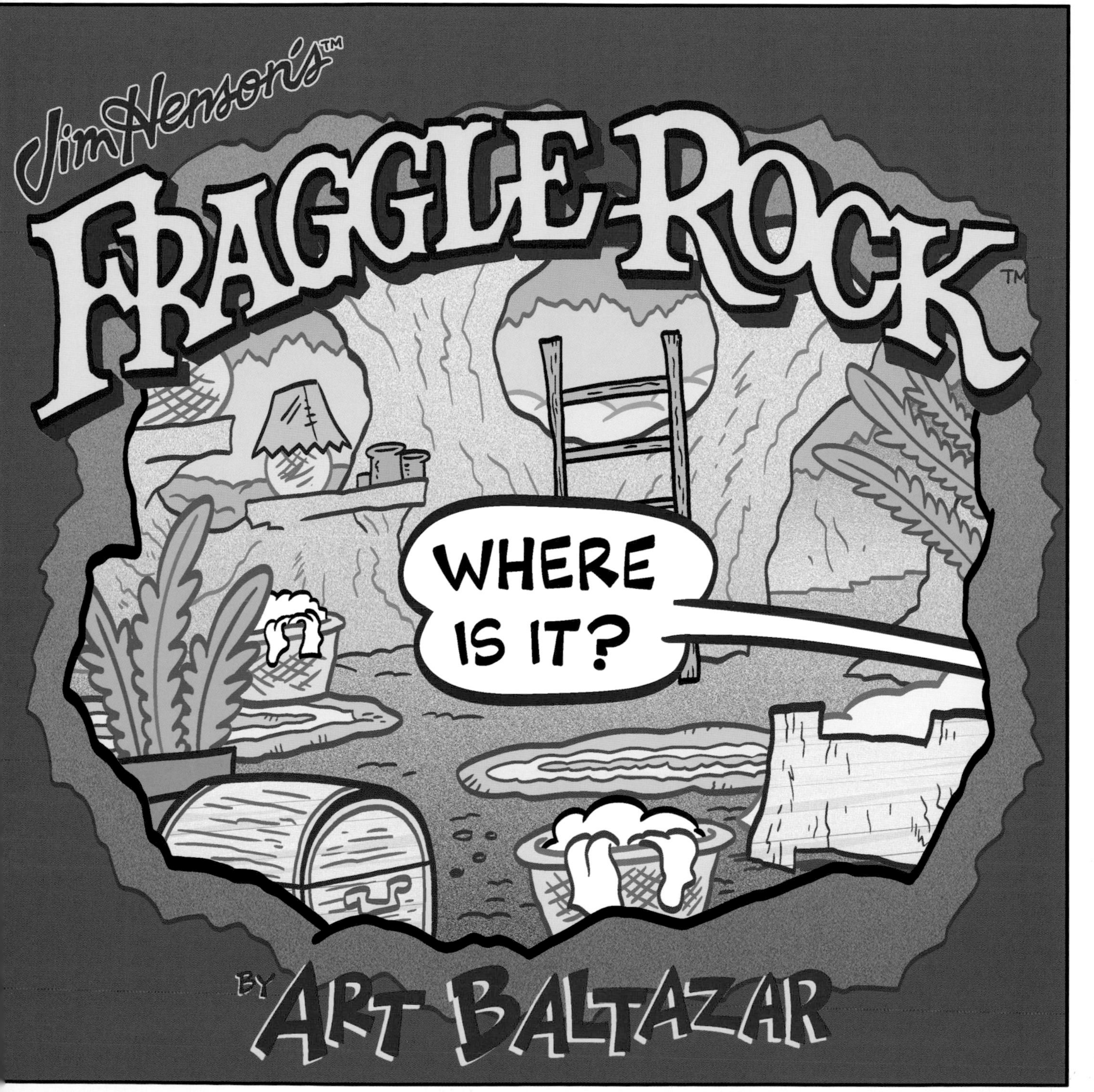
Jim Henson's™
FRAGGLE ROCK™
WHERE IS IT?
BY ART BALTAZAR

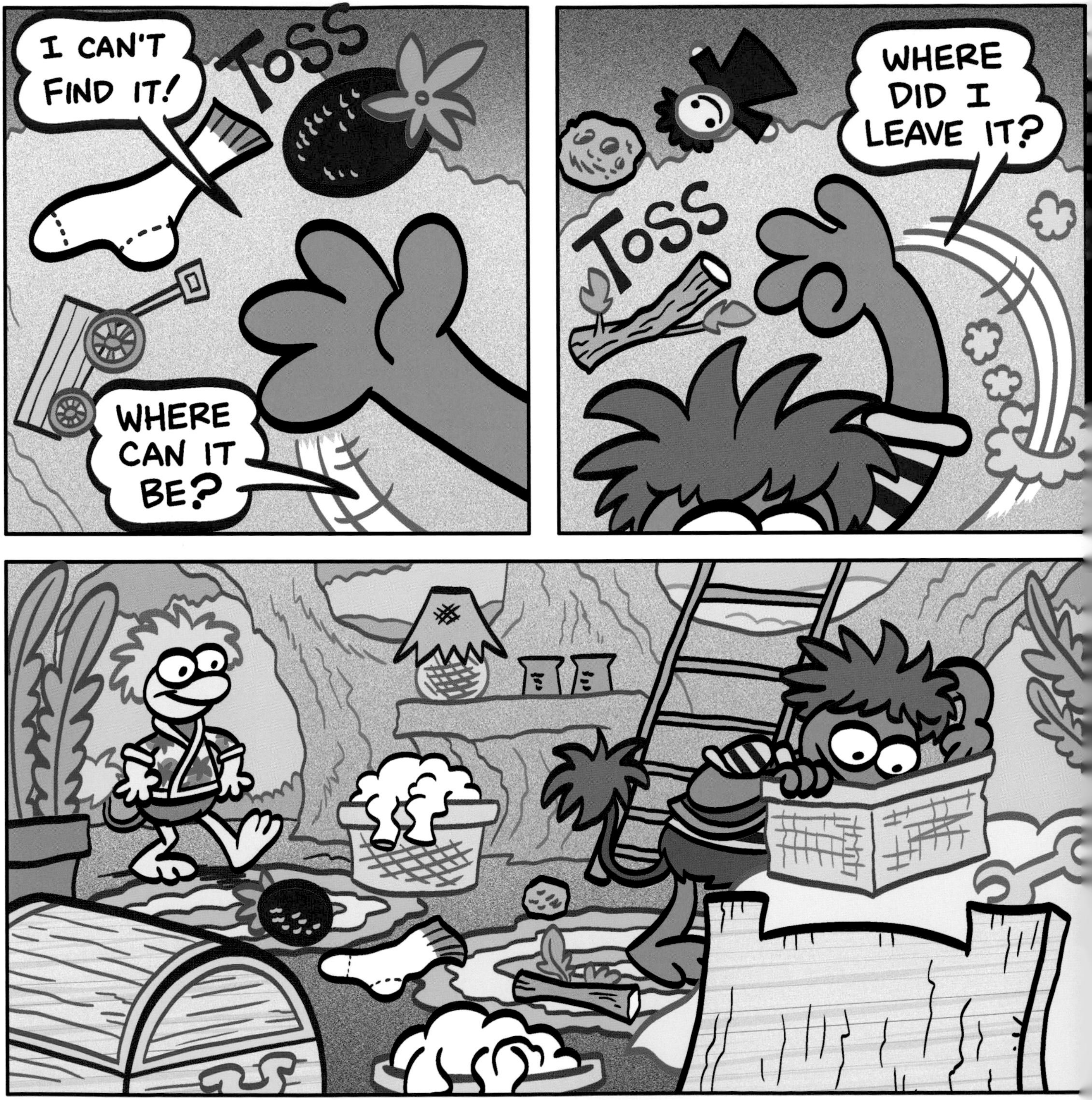
I CAN'T FIND IT!
TOSS
WHERE CAN IT BE?
WHERE DID I LEAVE IT?
TOSS

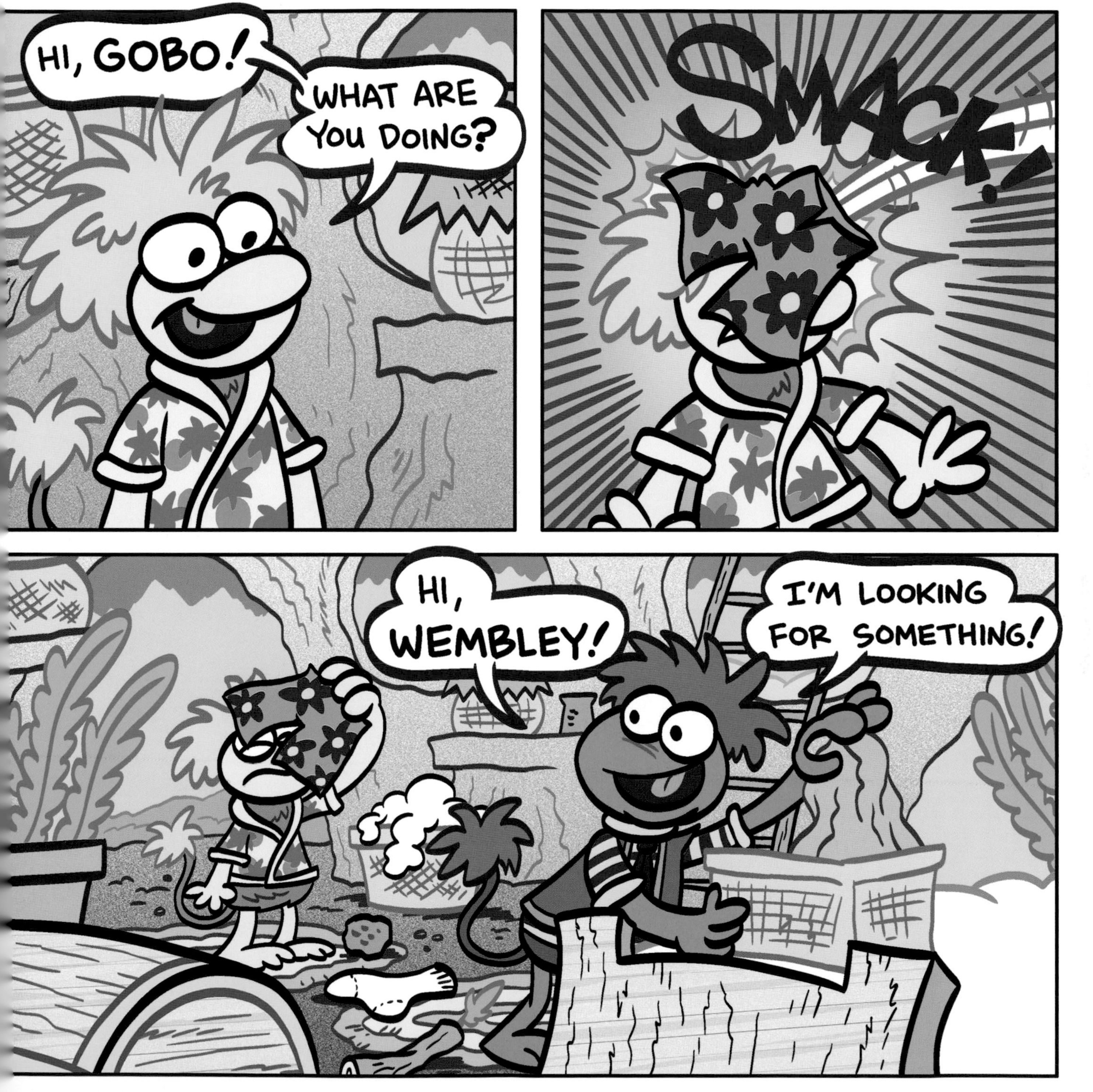
HI, GOBO!
WHAT ARE YOU DOING?
SMACK!
HI, WEMBLEY!
I'M LOOKING FOR SOMETHING!

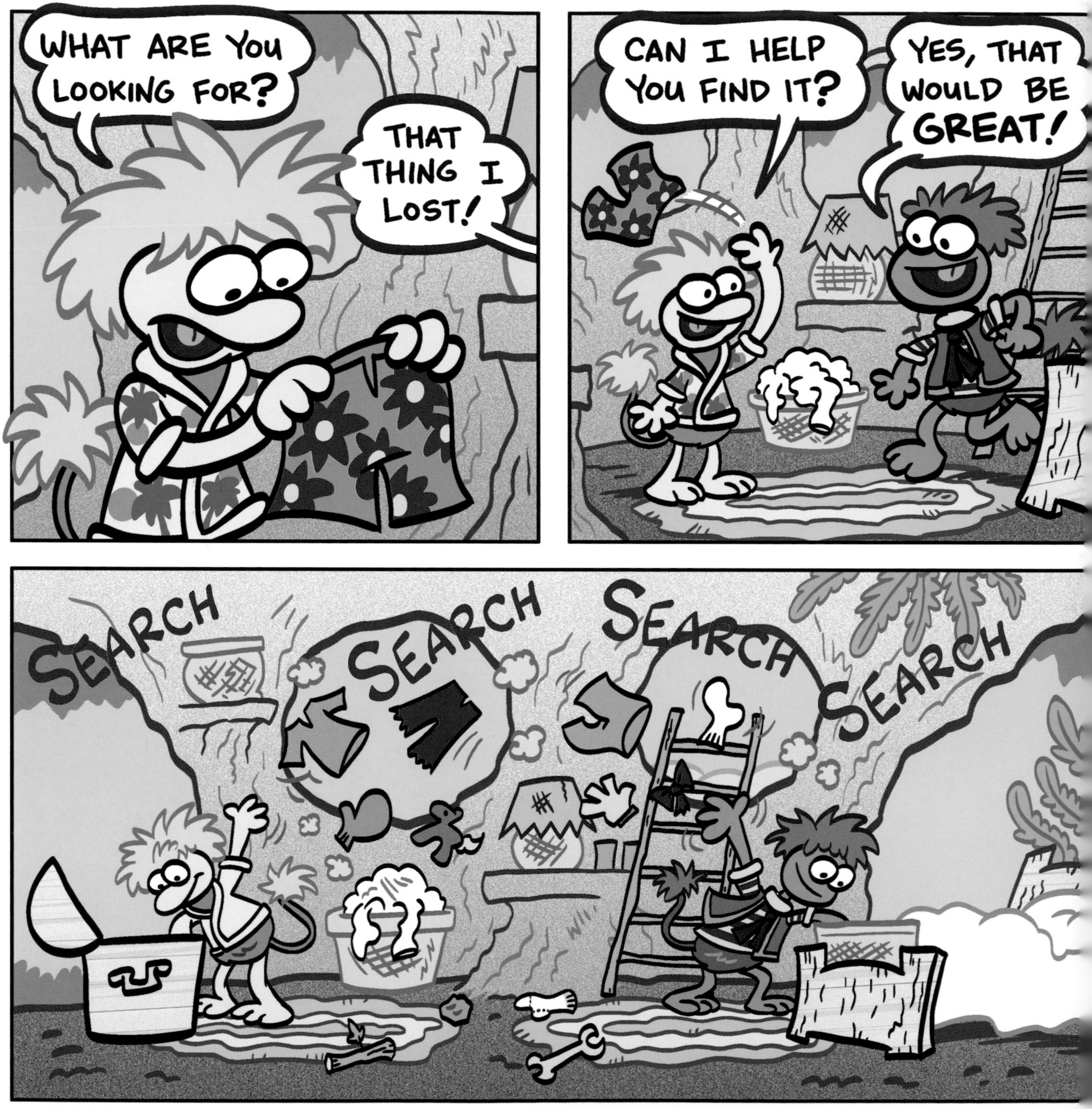
WHAT ARE YOU LOOKING FOR?
THAT THING I LOST!
CAN I HELP YOU FIND IT?
YES, THAT WOULD BE GREAT!
SEARCH
SEARCH
SEARCH
SEARCH

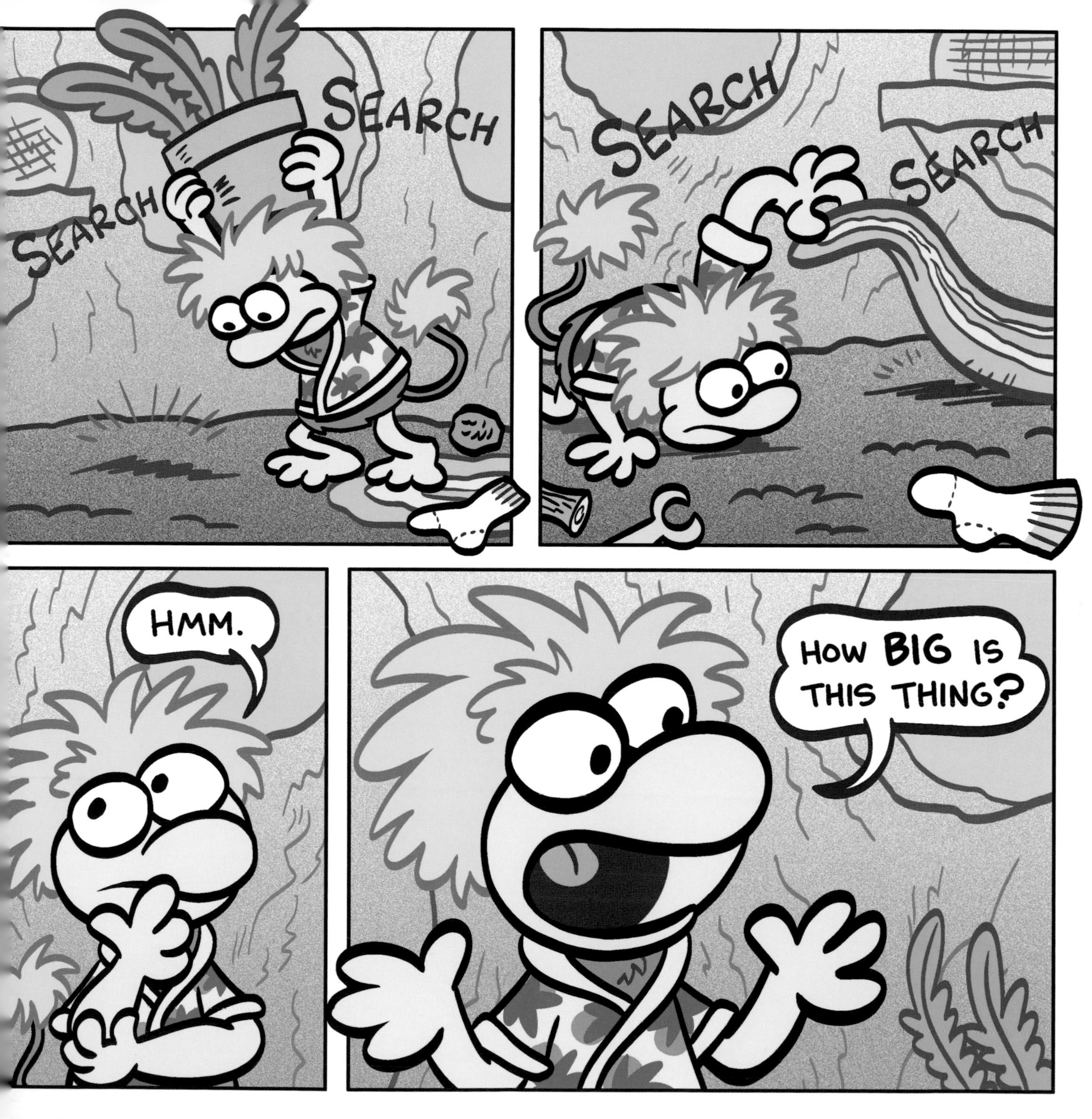
SEARCH
SEARCH
SEARCH
SEARCH
HMM.
HOW BIG IS THIS THING?

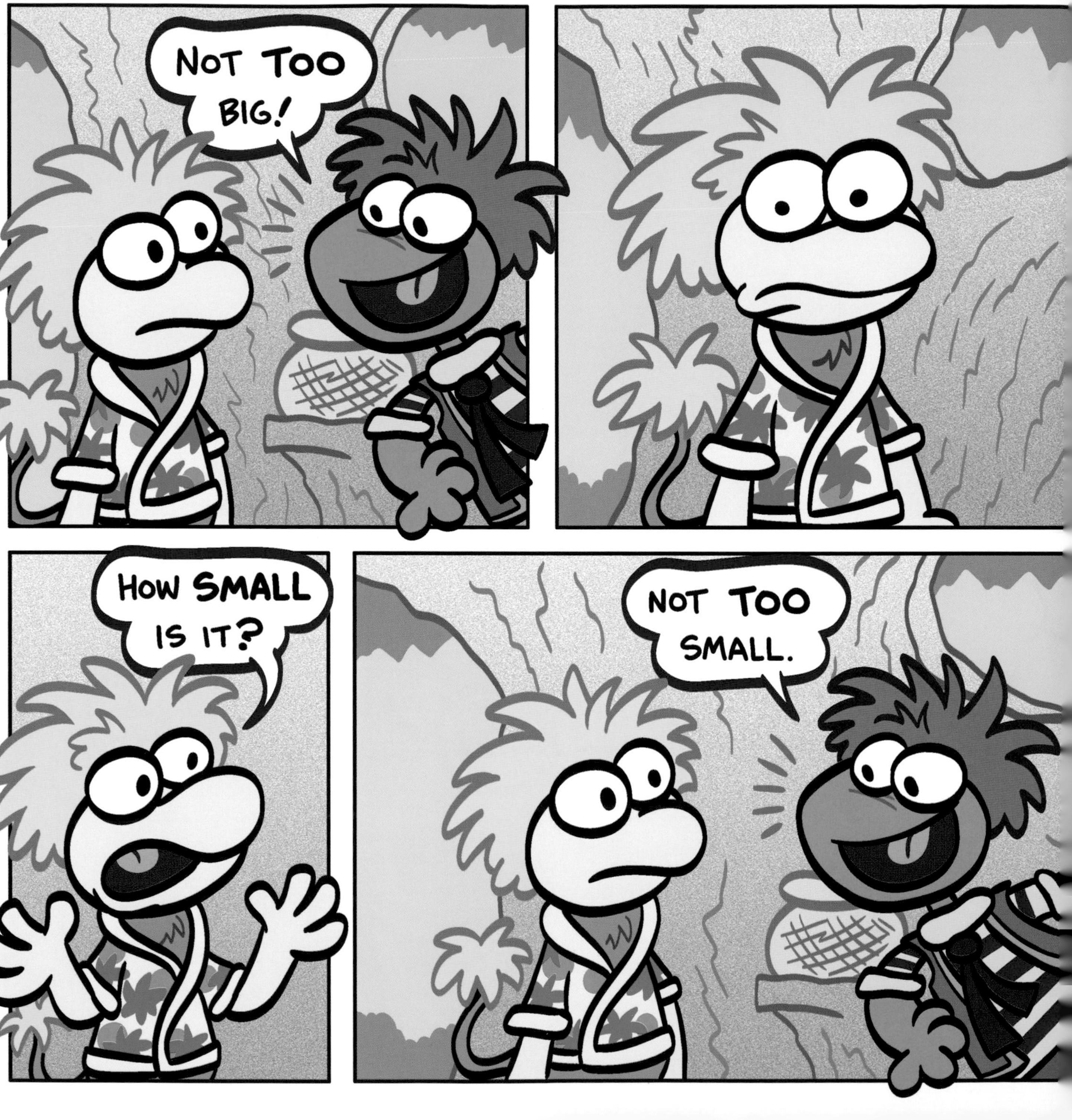
NOT TOO BIG!
HOW SMALL IS IT?
NOT TOO SMALL.

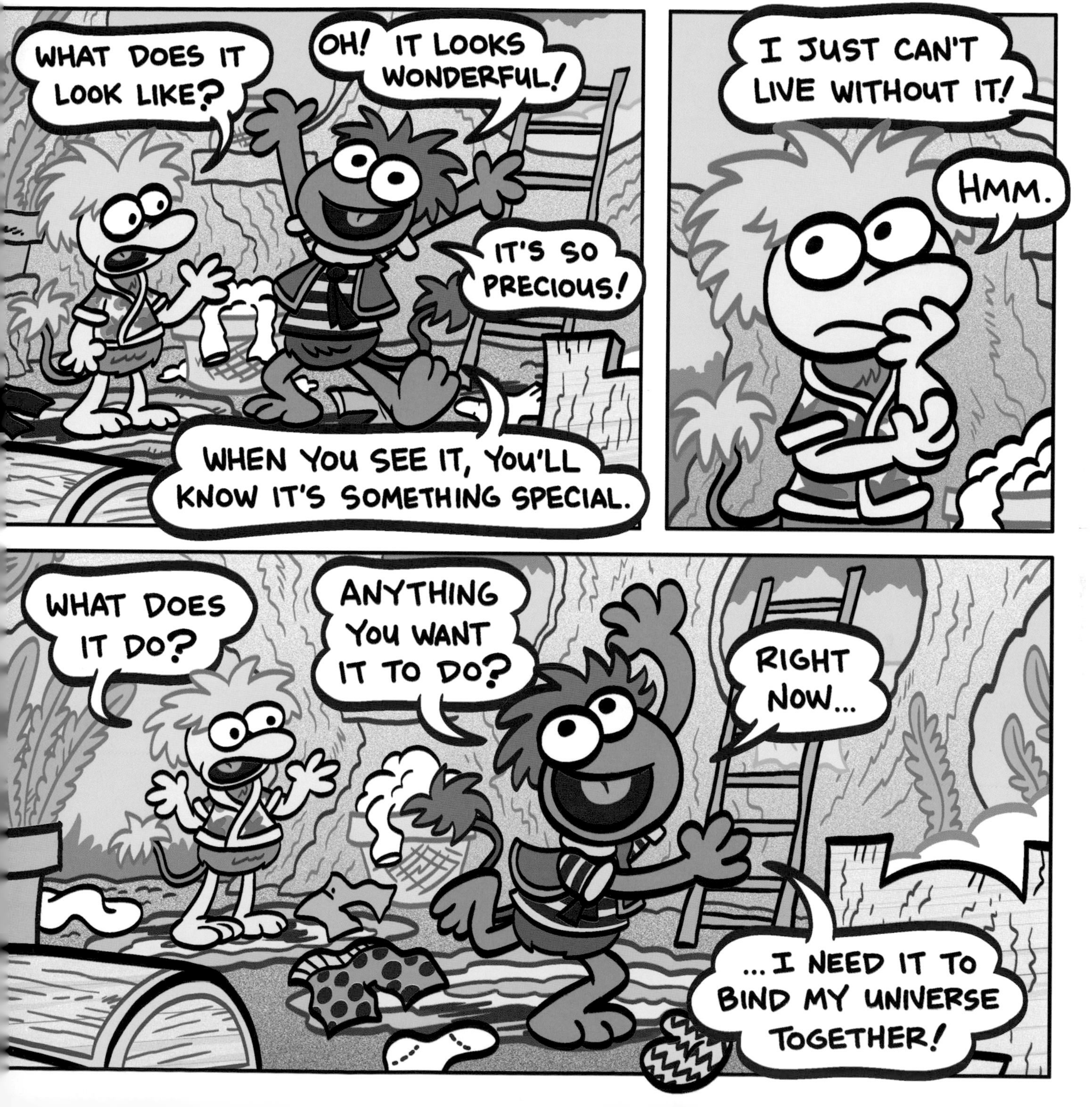
WHAT DOES IT LOOK LIKE?
OH! IT LOOKS WONDERFUL!
IT'S SO PRECIOUS!
WHEN YOU SEE IT, YOU'LL KNOW IT'S SOMETHING SPECIAL.
I JUST CAN'T LIVE WITHOUT IT!
HMM.
WHAT DOES IT DO?
ANYTHING YOU WANT IT TO DO?
RIGHT NOW...
...I NEED IT TO BIND MY UNIVERSE TOGETHER!

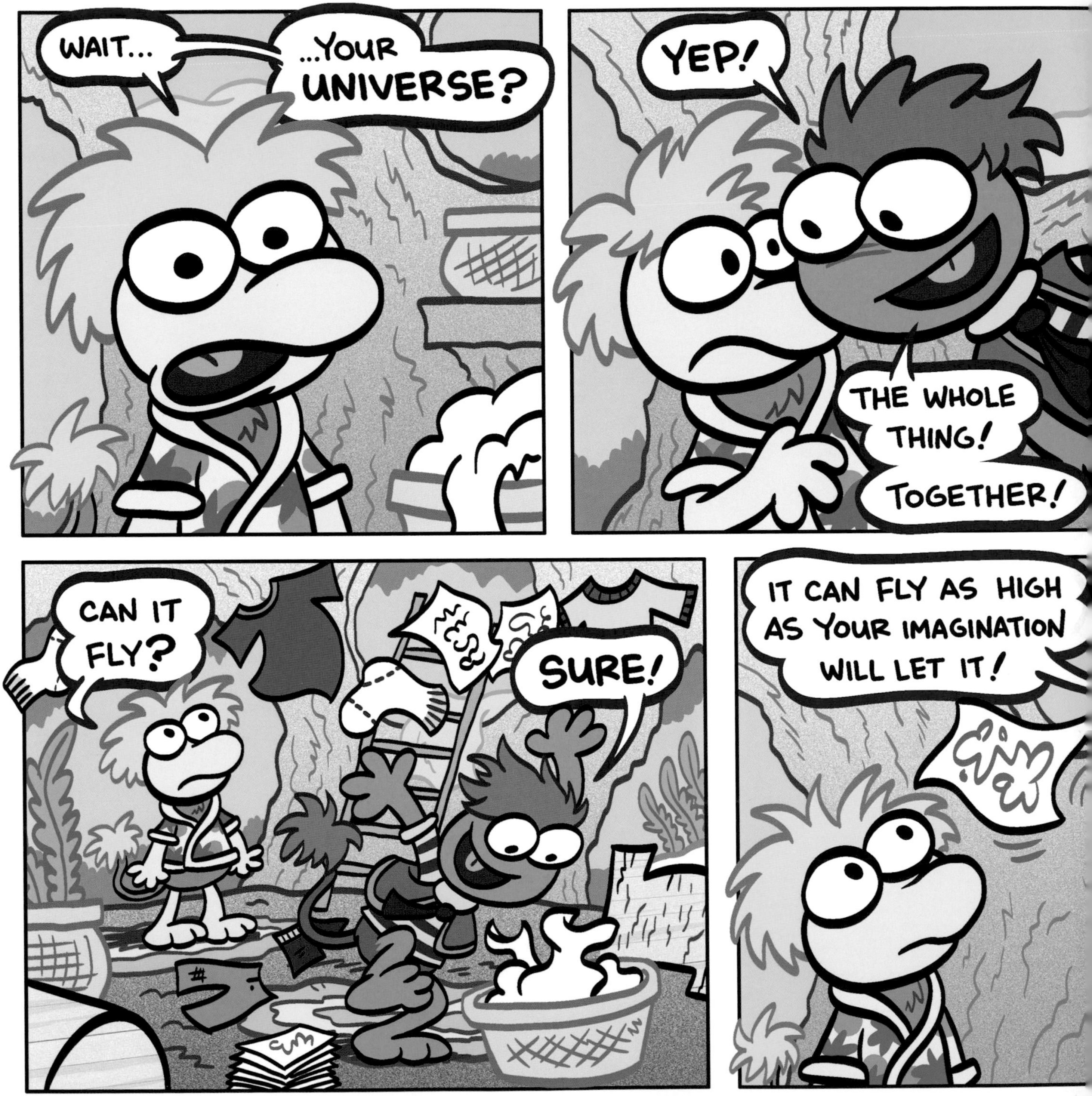
WAIT...
...YOUR UNIVERSE?
YEP!
THE WHOLE THING!
TOGETHER!
CAN IT FLY?
SURE!
IT CAN FLY AS HIGH AS YOUR IMAGINATION WILL LET IT!

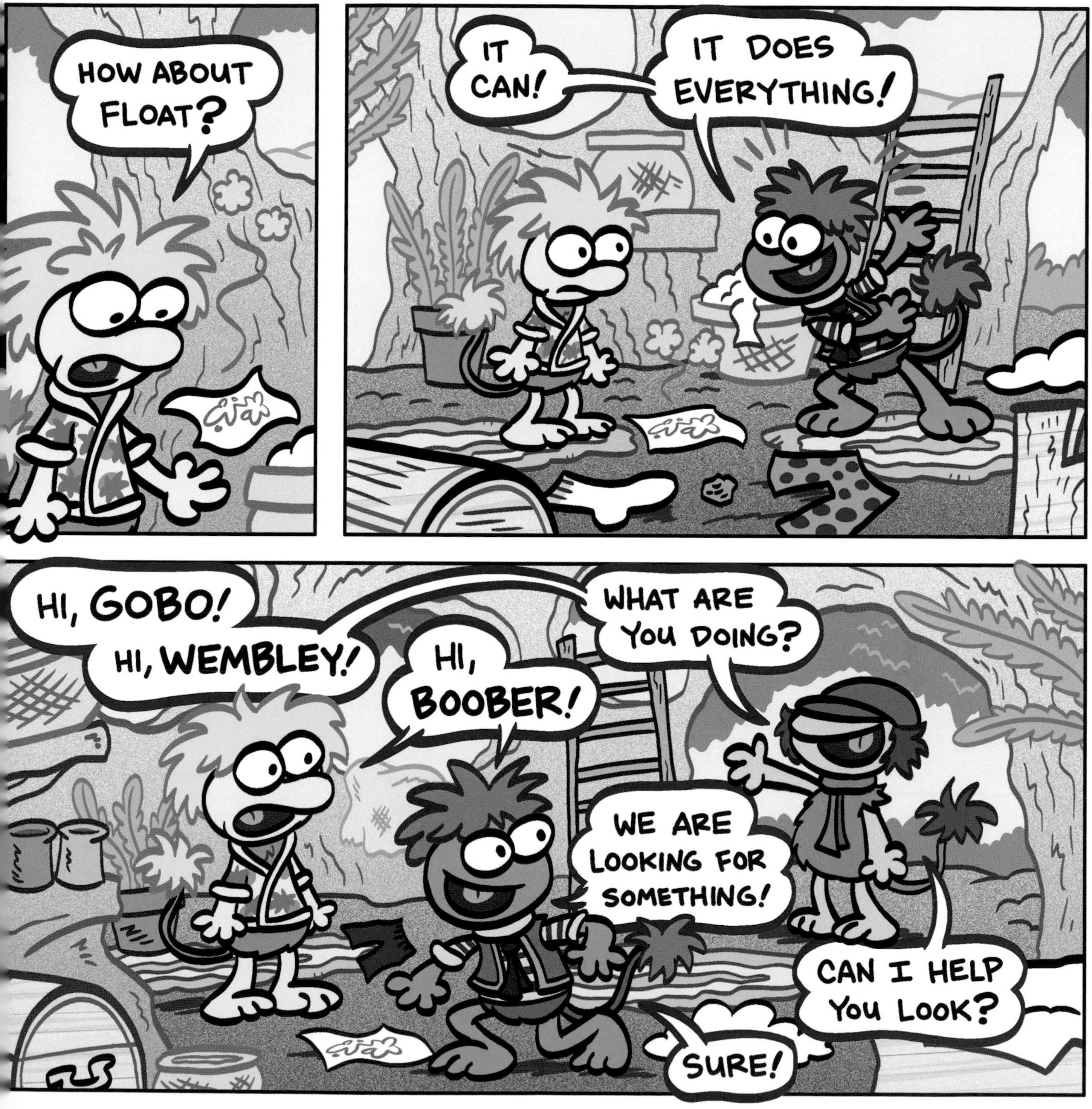
HOW ABOUT FLOAT?
IT CAN!
IT DOES EVERYTHING!
HI, GOBO!
HI, WEMBLEY!
HI, BOOBER!
WHAT ARE YOU DOING?
WE ARE LOOKING FOR SOMETHING!
CAN I HELP YOU LOOK?
SURE!

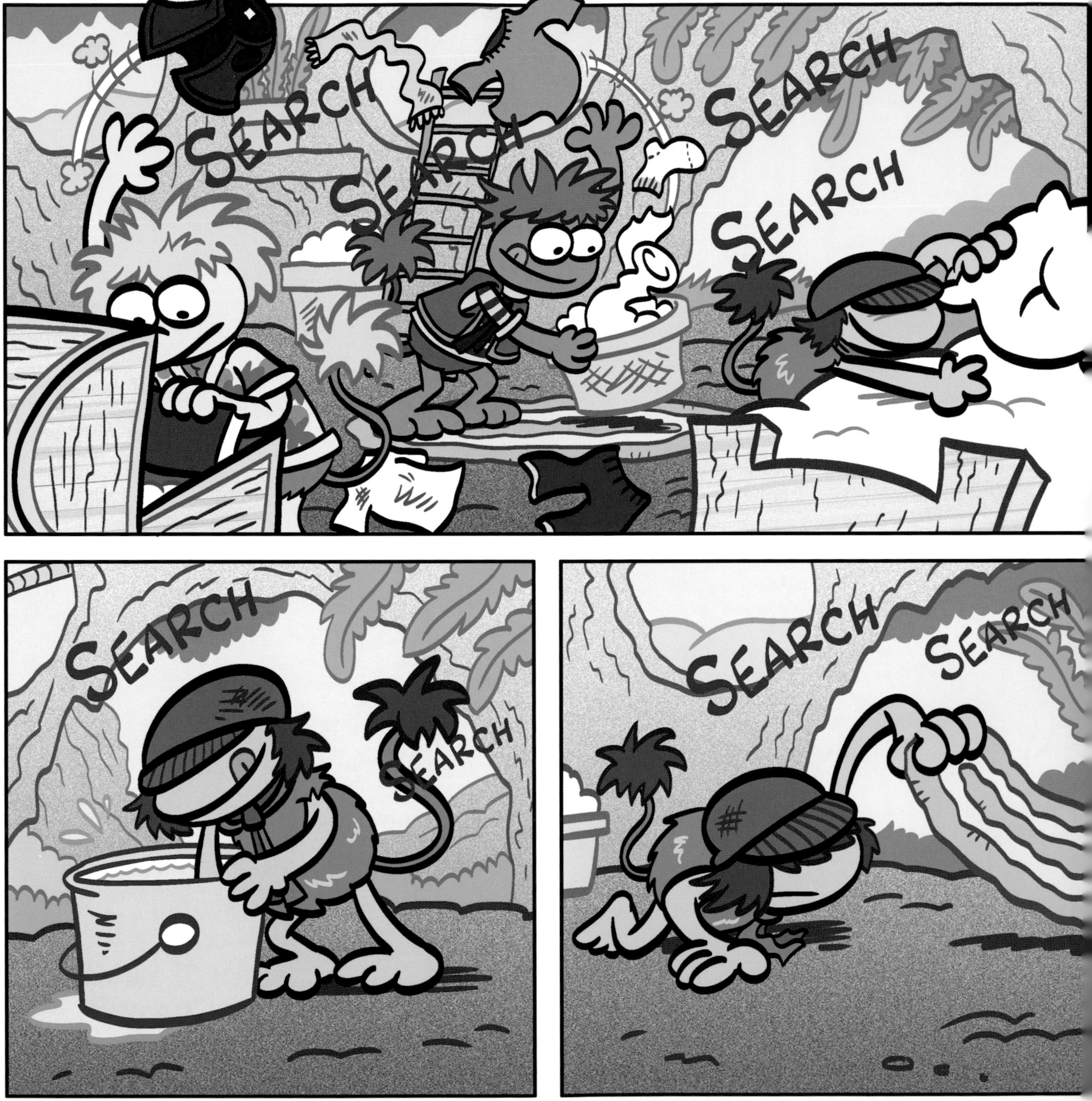
SEARCH
SEARCH
SEARCH
SEARCH
SEARCH
SEARCH
SEARCH
SEARCH

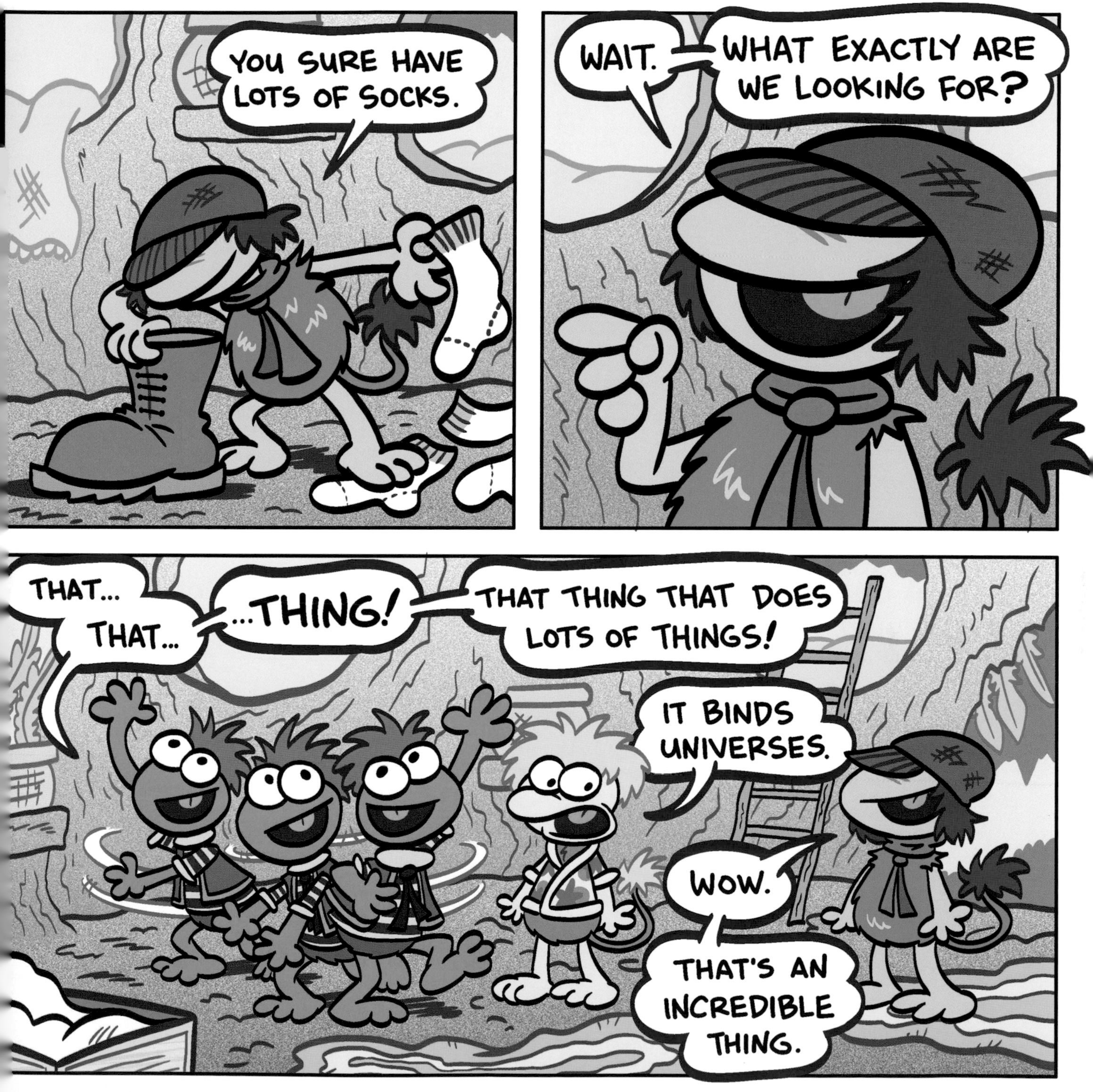
YOU SURE HAVE LOTS OF SOCKS.
WAIT.
WHAT EXACTLY ARE WE LOOKING FOR?
THAT... THAT...
...THING!
THAT THING THAT DOES LOTS OF THINGS!
IT BINDS UNIVERSES.
WOW.
THAT'S AN INCREDIBLE THING.

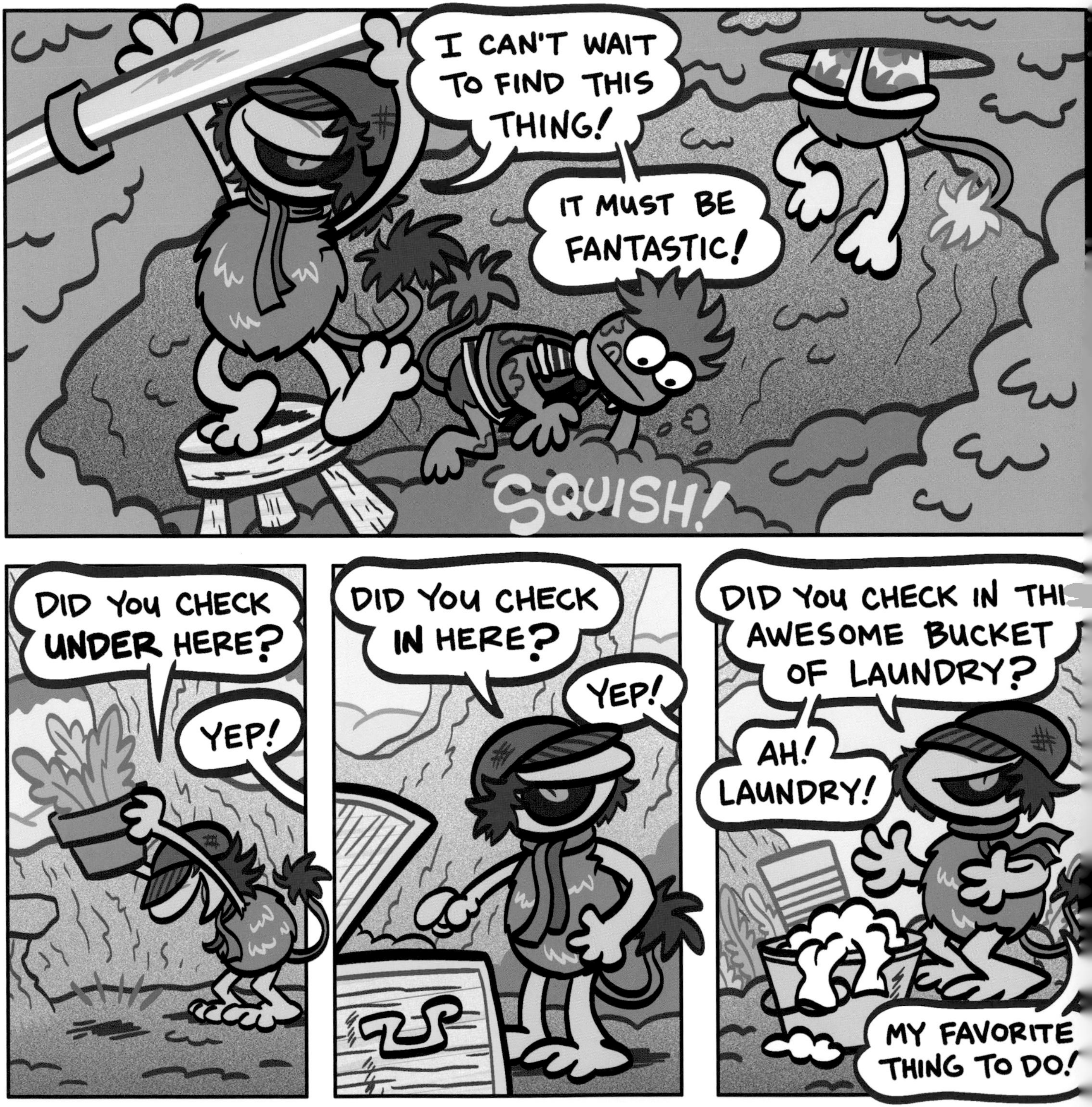
I CAN'T WAIT TO FIND THIS THING!
IT MUST BE FANTASTIC!
SQUISH!
DID YOU CHECK UNDER HERE?
YEP!
DID YOU CHECK IN HERE?
YEP!
DID YOU CHECK IN THIS AWESOME BUCKET OF LAUNDRY?
AH! LAUNDRY!
MY FAVORITE THING TO DO!

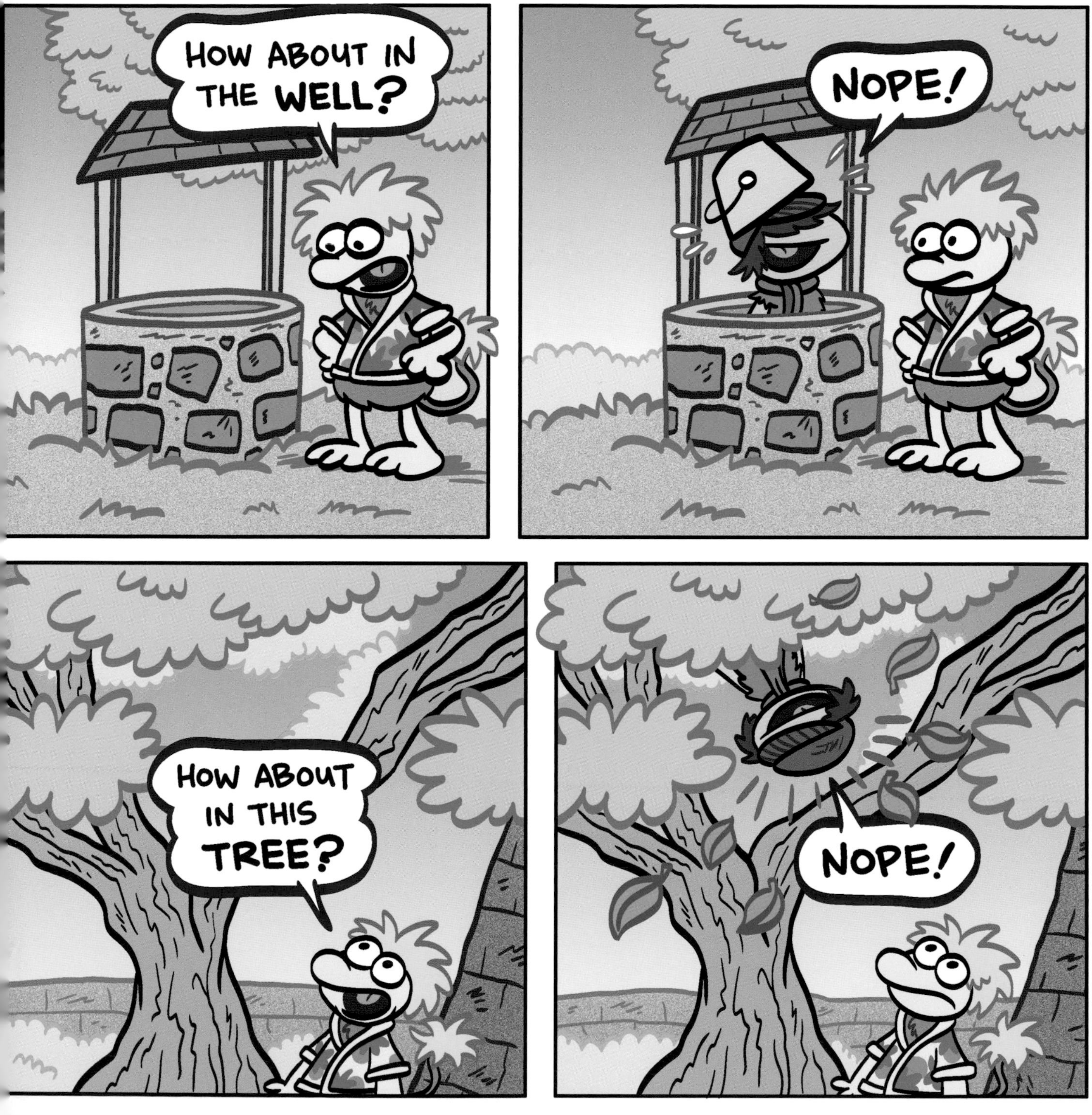
HOW ABOUT IN THE WELL?
NOPE!
HOW ABOUT IN THIS TREE?
NOPE!

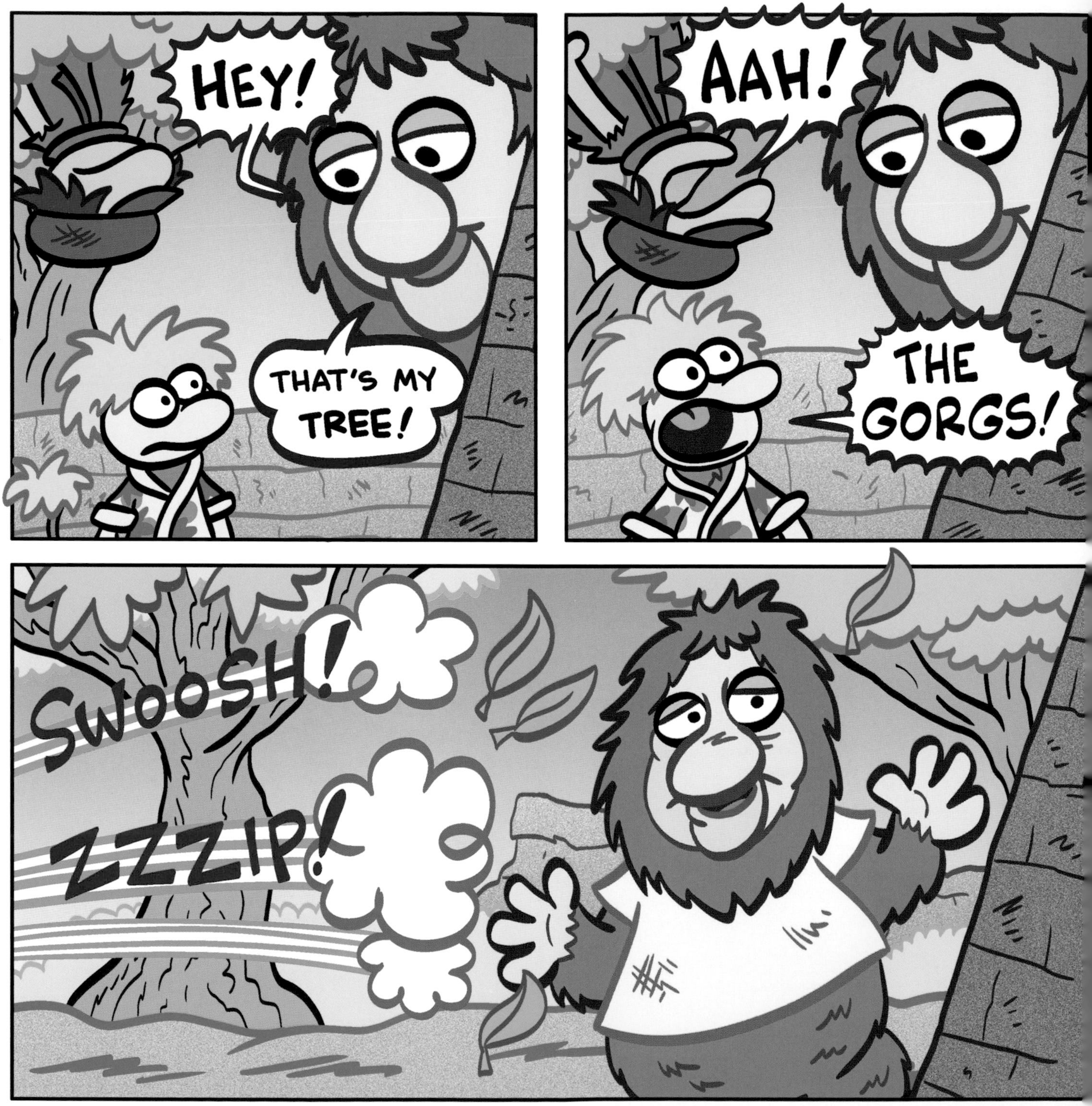
HEY!
THAT'S MY TREE!
AAH!
THE GORGS!
SWOOSH!
ZZZIP!

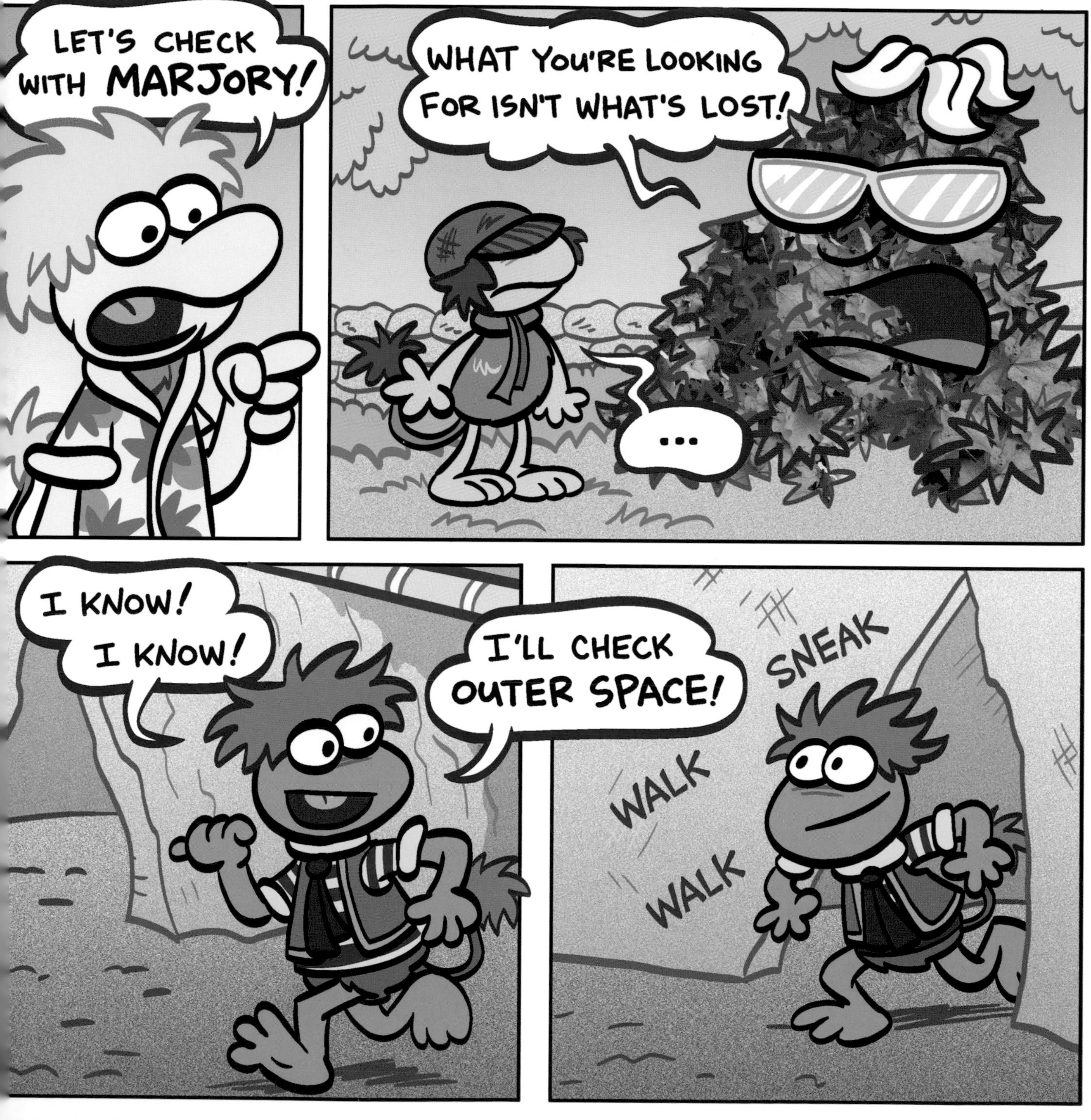
LET'S CHECK WITH MARJORY!
WHAT YOU'RE LOOKING FOR ISN'T WHAT'S LOST!
...
I KNOW! I KNOW!
I'LL CHECK OUTER SPACE!
SNEAK
WALK
WALK

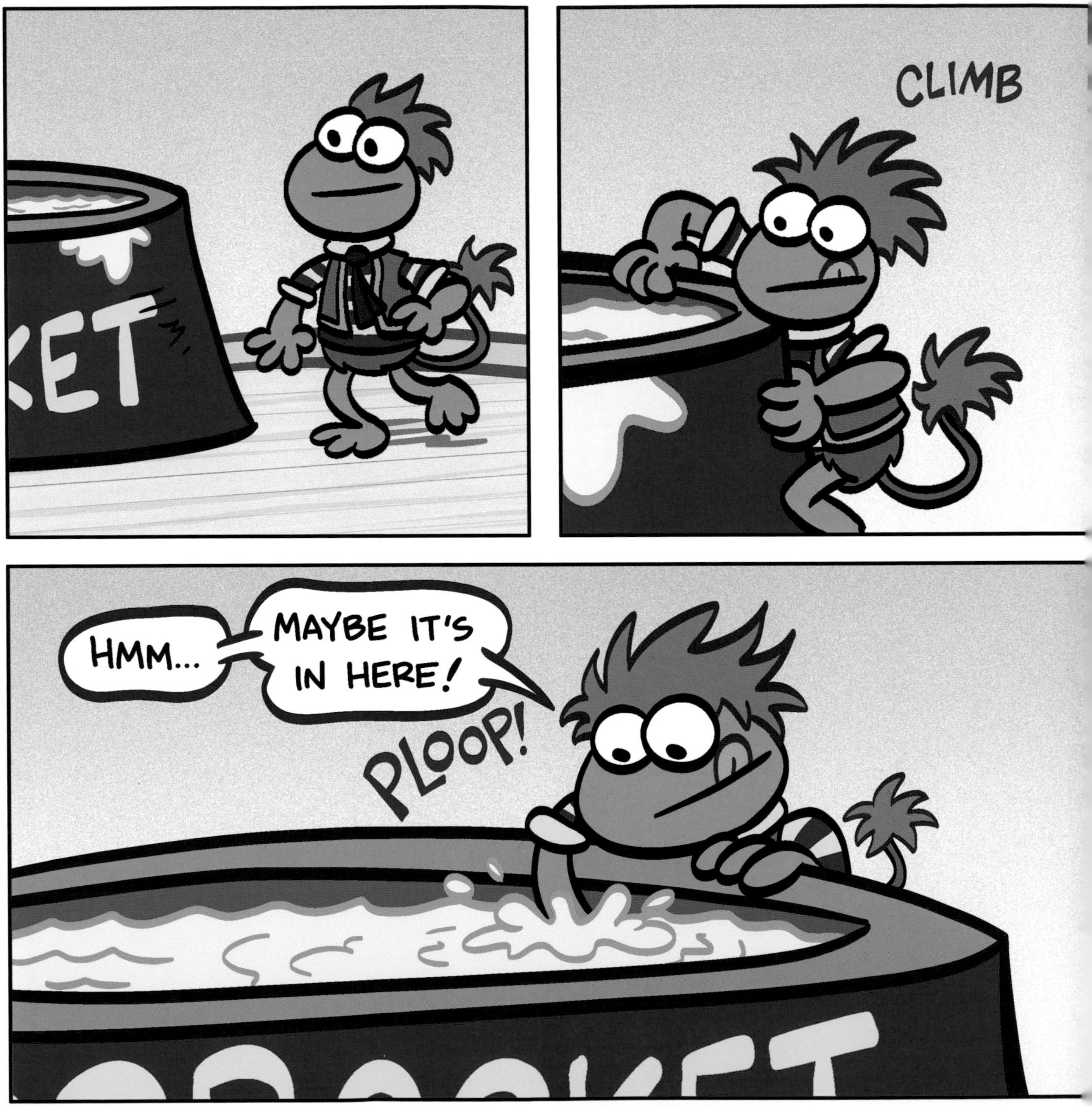

KET
CLIMB
HMM...
MAYBE IT'S IN HERE!
PLOOP!

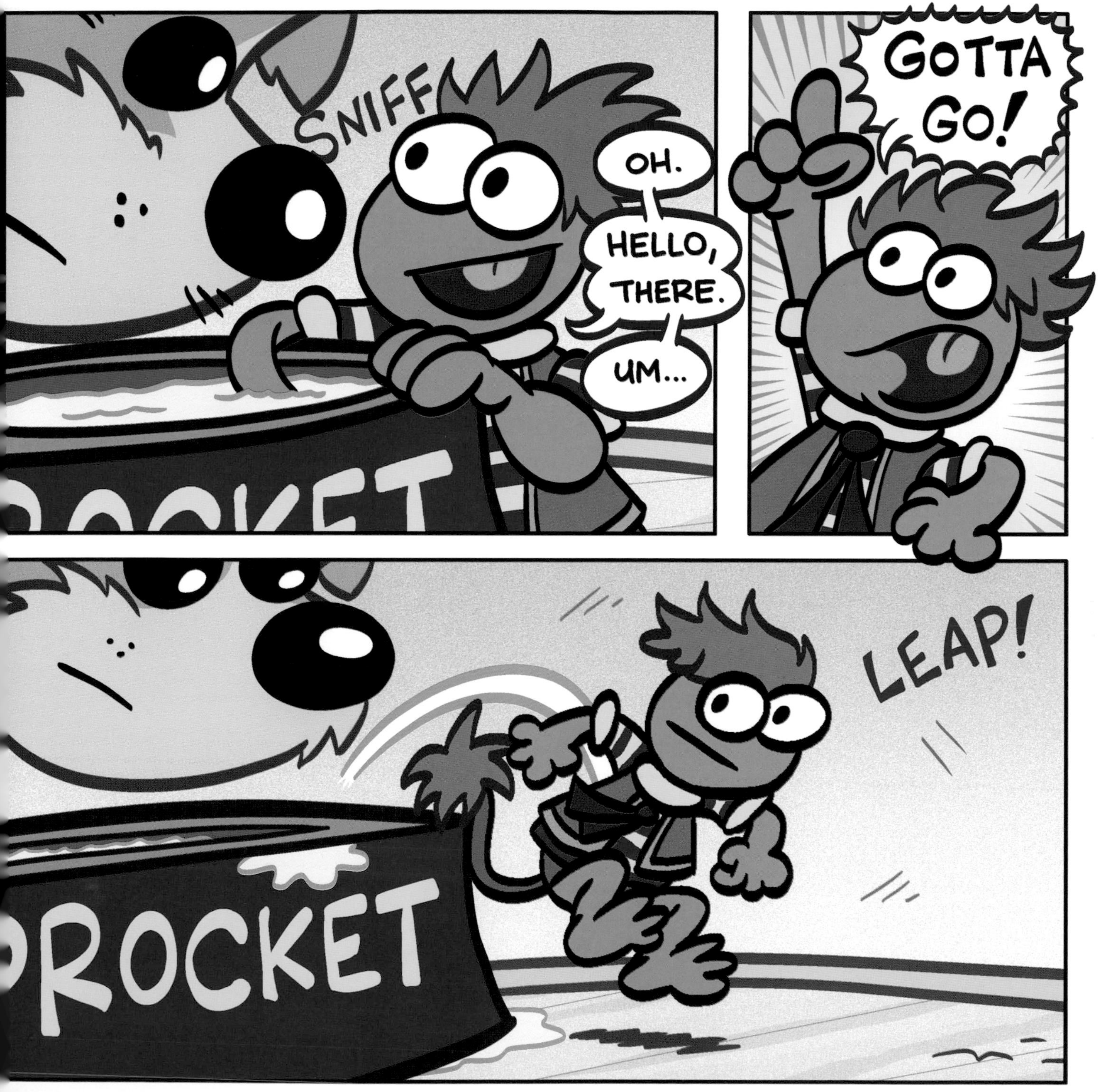
SNIFF
OH.
HELLO, THERE.
UM...
ROCKET
GOTTA GO!
LEAP!
ROCKET

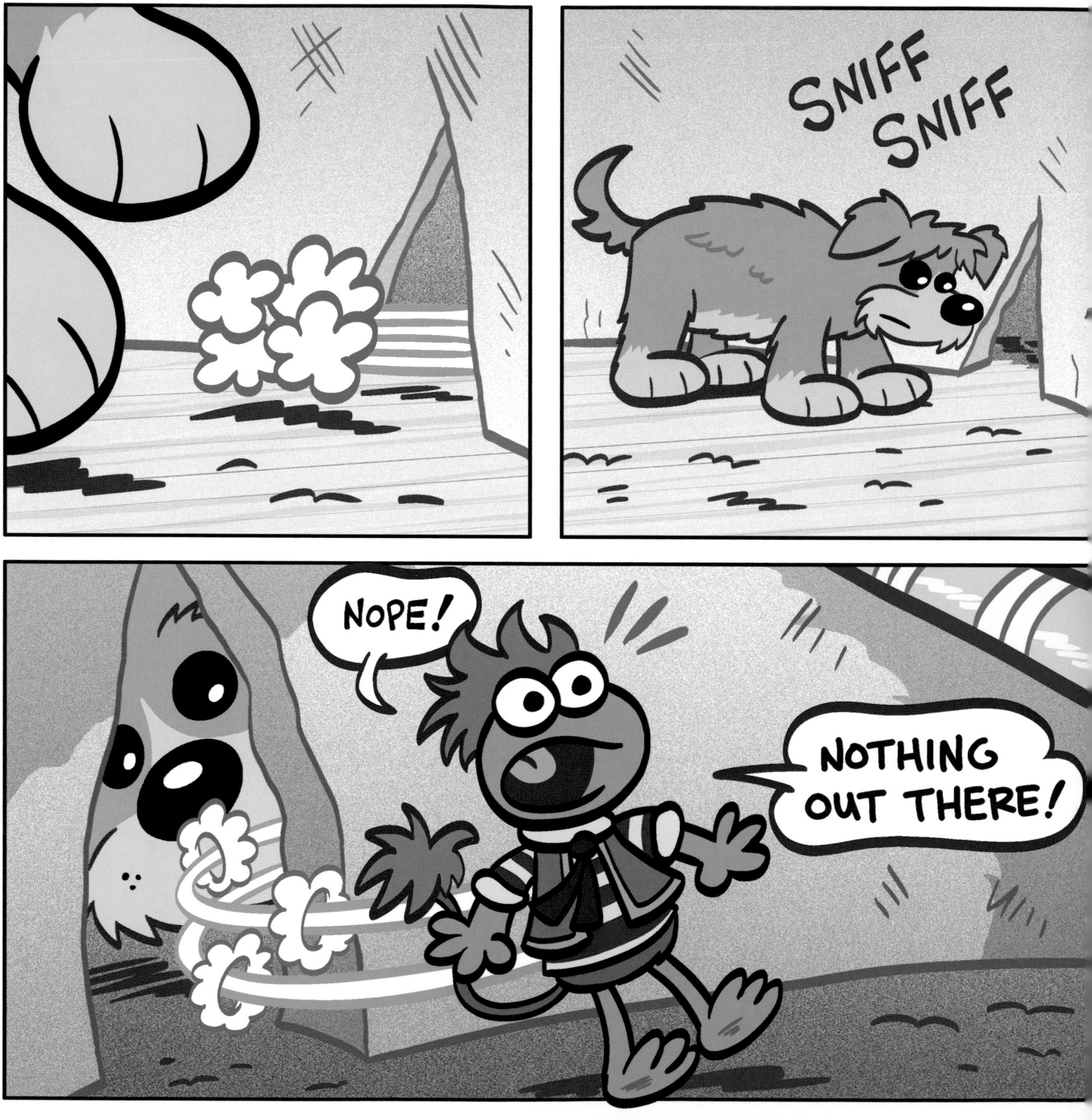
SNIFF
SNIFF
NOPE!
NOTHING OUT THERE!

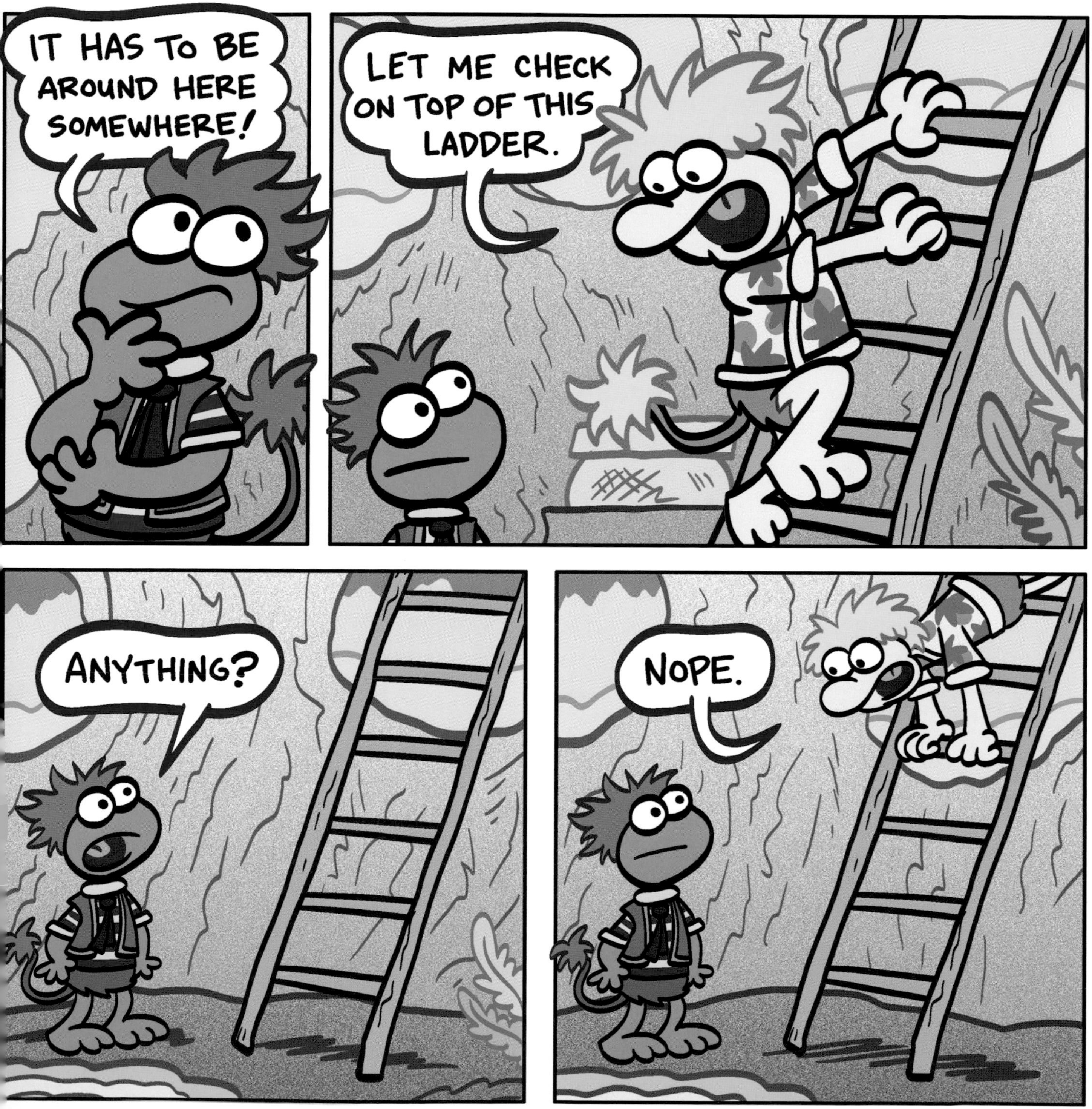
IT HAS TO BE AROUND HERE SOMEWHERE!
LET ME CHECK ON TOP OF THIS LADDER.
ANYTHING?
NOPE.

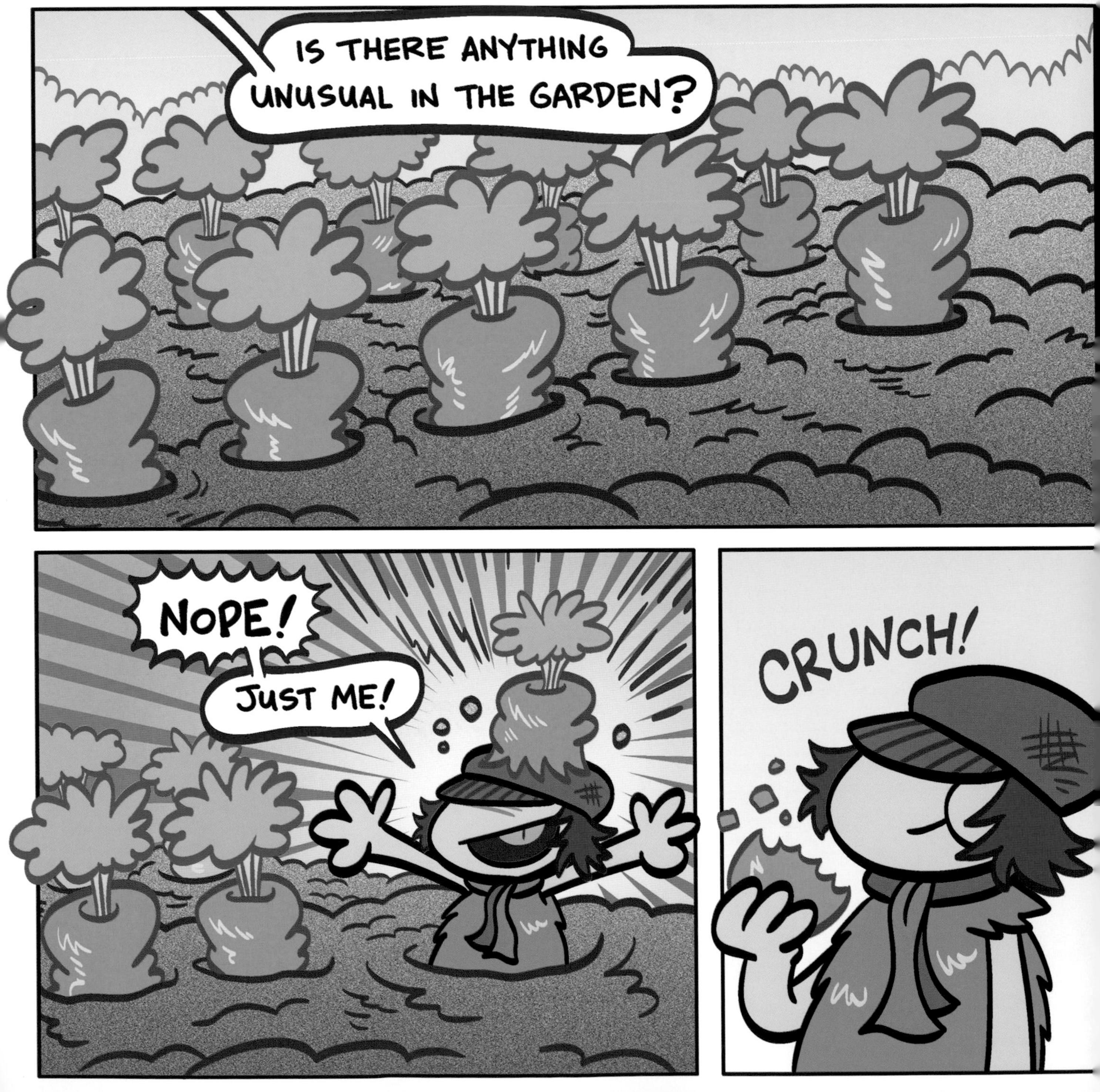
IS THERE ANYTHING UNUSUAL IN THE GARDEN?
NOPE!
JUST ME!
CRUNCH!

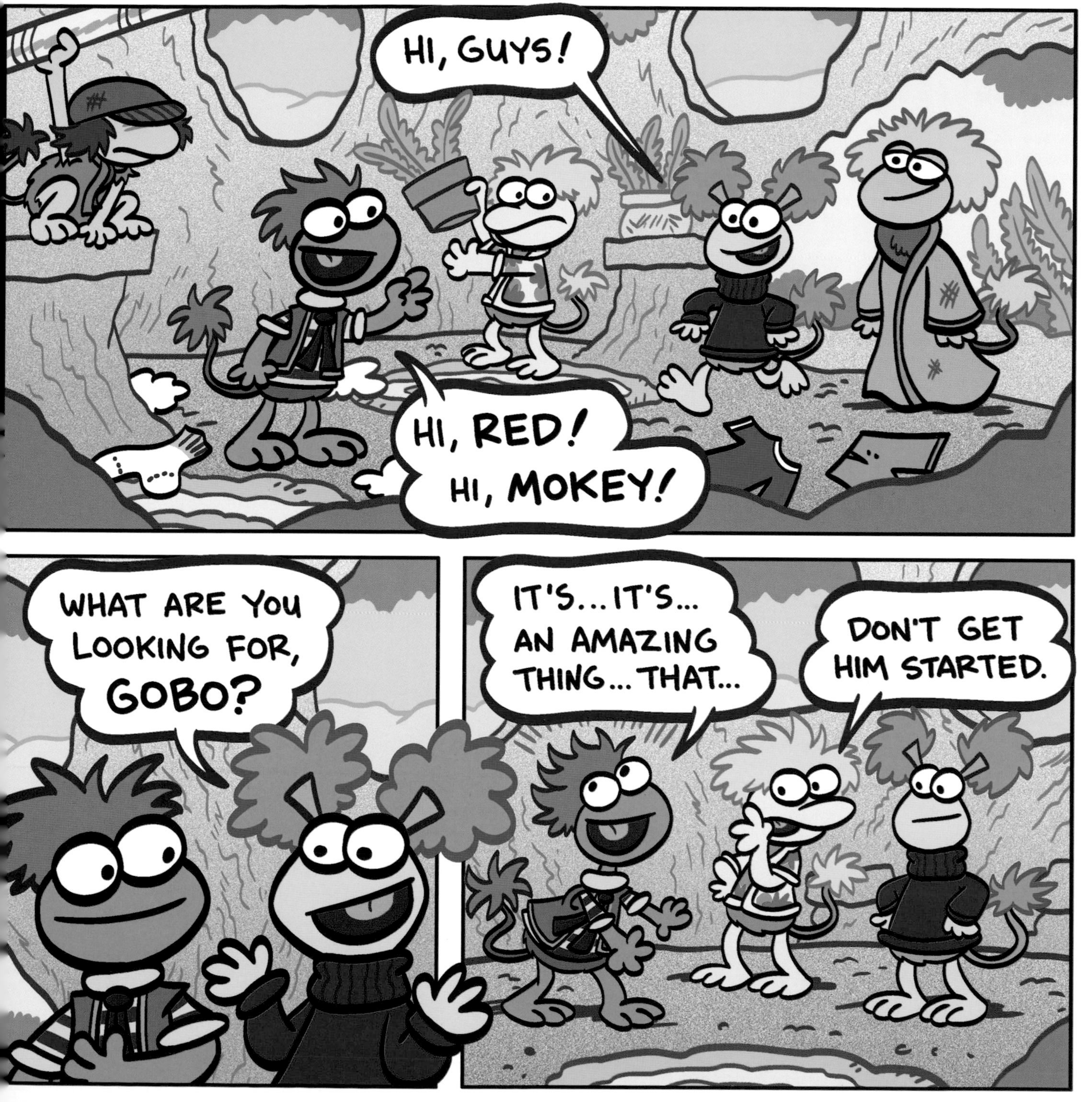
HI, GUYS!
HI, RED!
HI, MOKEY!
WHAT ARE YOU LOOKING FOR, GOBO?
IT'S... IT'S... AN AMAZING THING... THAT...
DON'T GET HIM STARTED.

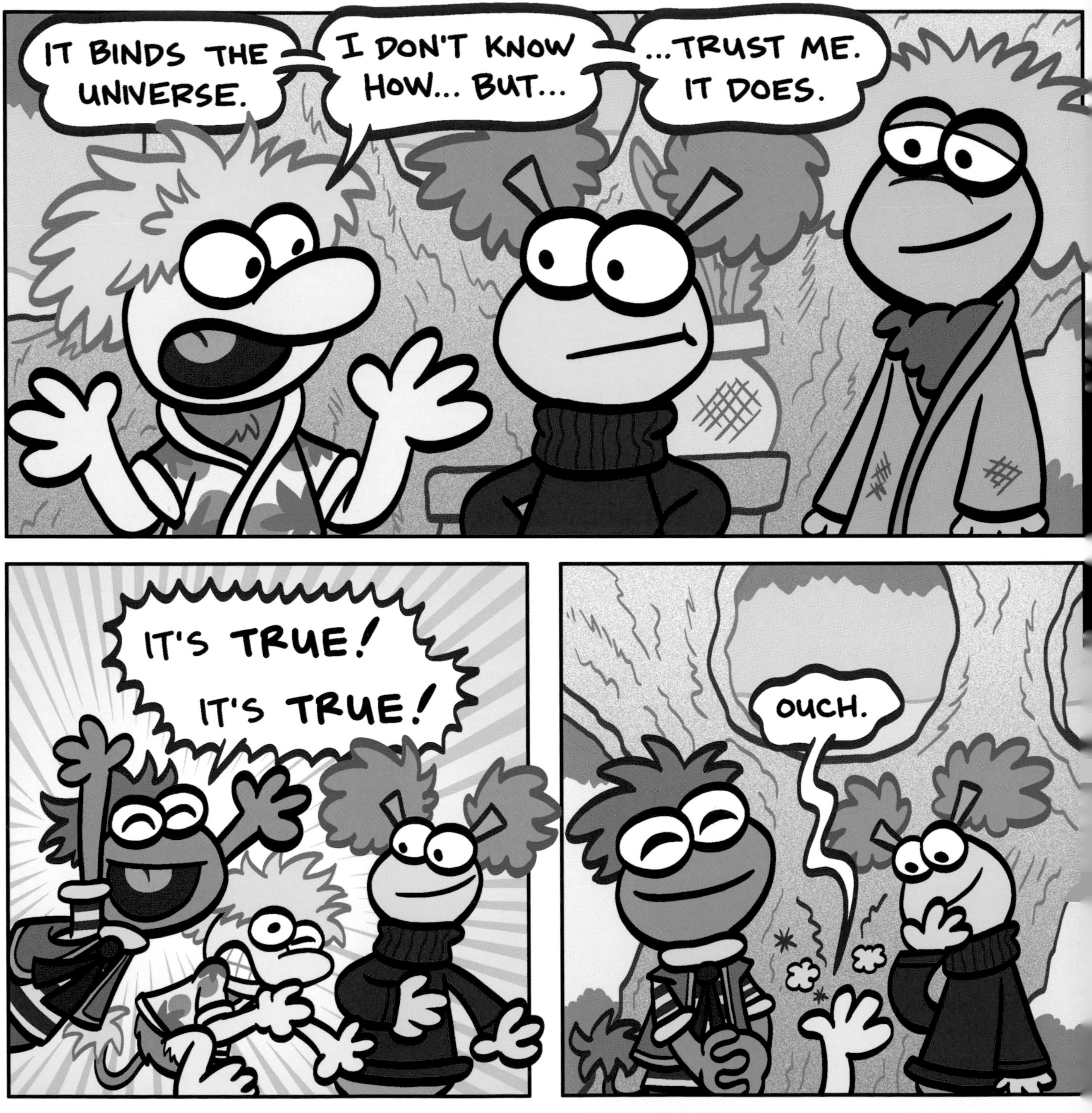
IT BINDS THE UNIVERSE.
I DON'T KNOW HOW... BUT...
...TRUST ME. IT DOES.
IT'S TRUE!
IT'S TRUE!
OUCH.

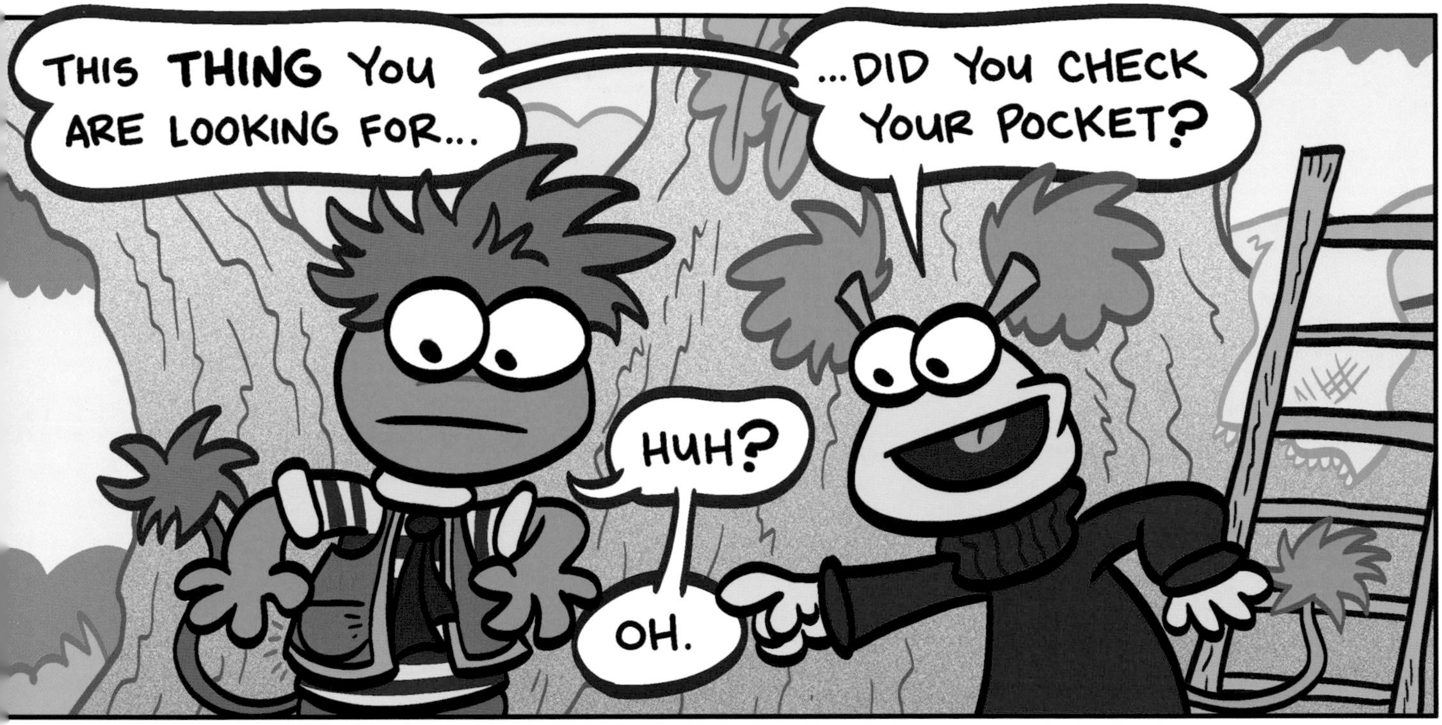
THIS THING YOU ARE LOOKING FOR...
...DID YOU CHECK YOUR POCKET?
HUH?
OH.

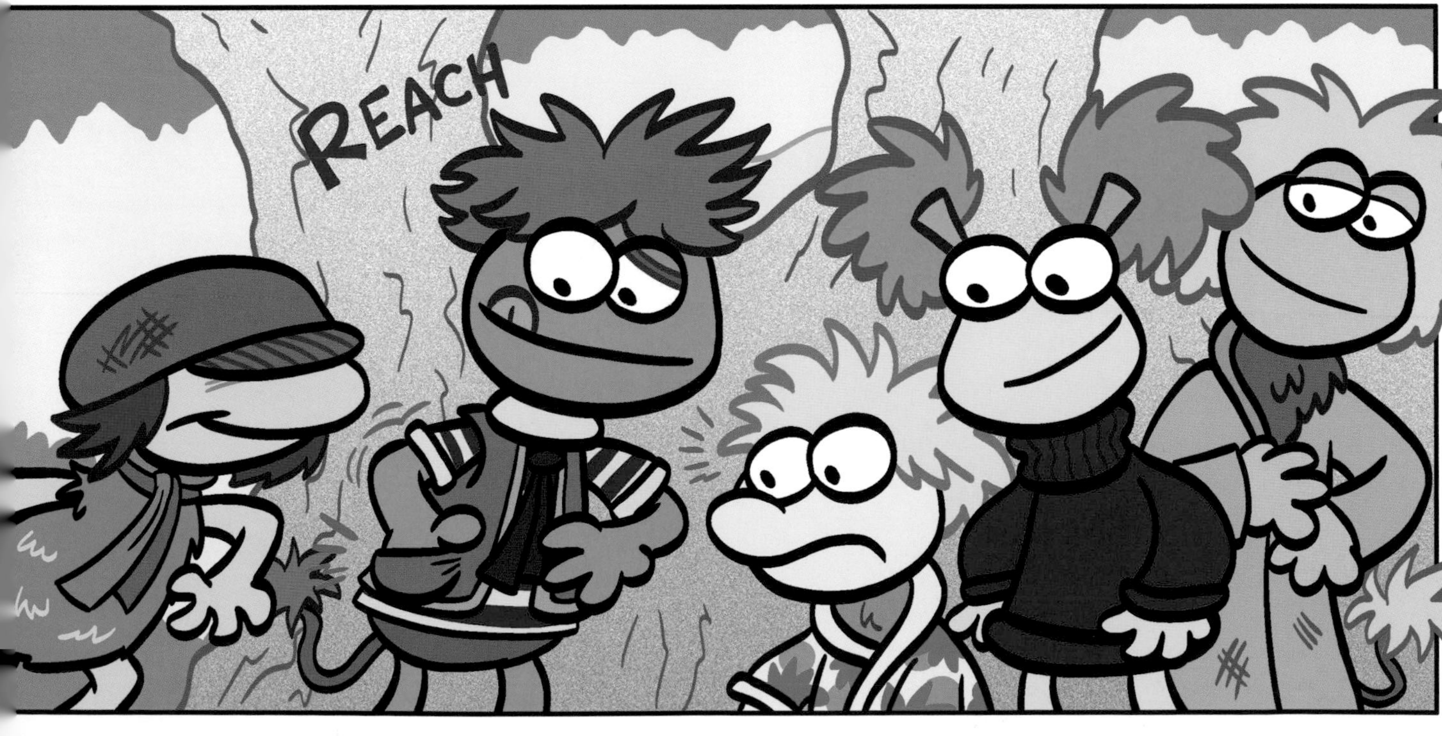
REACH

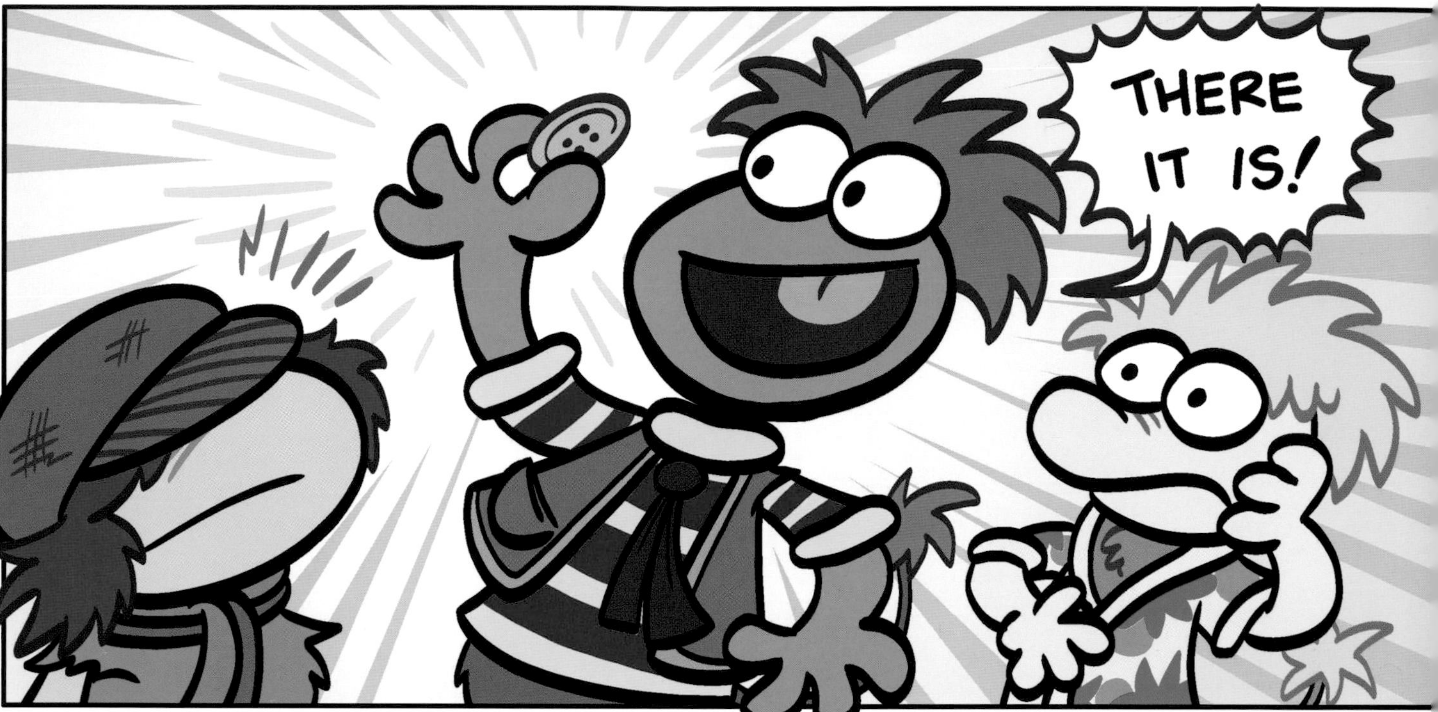
THERE IT IS!

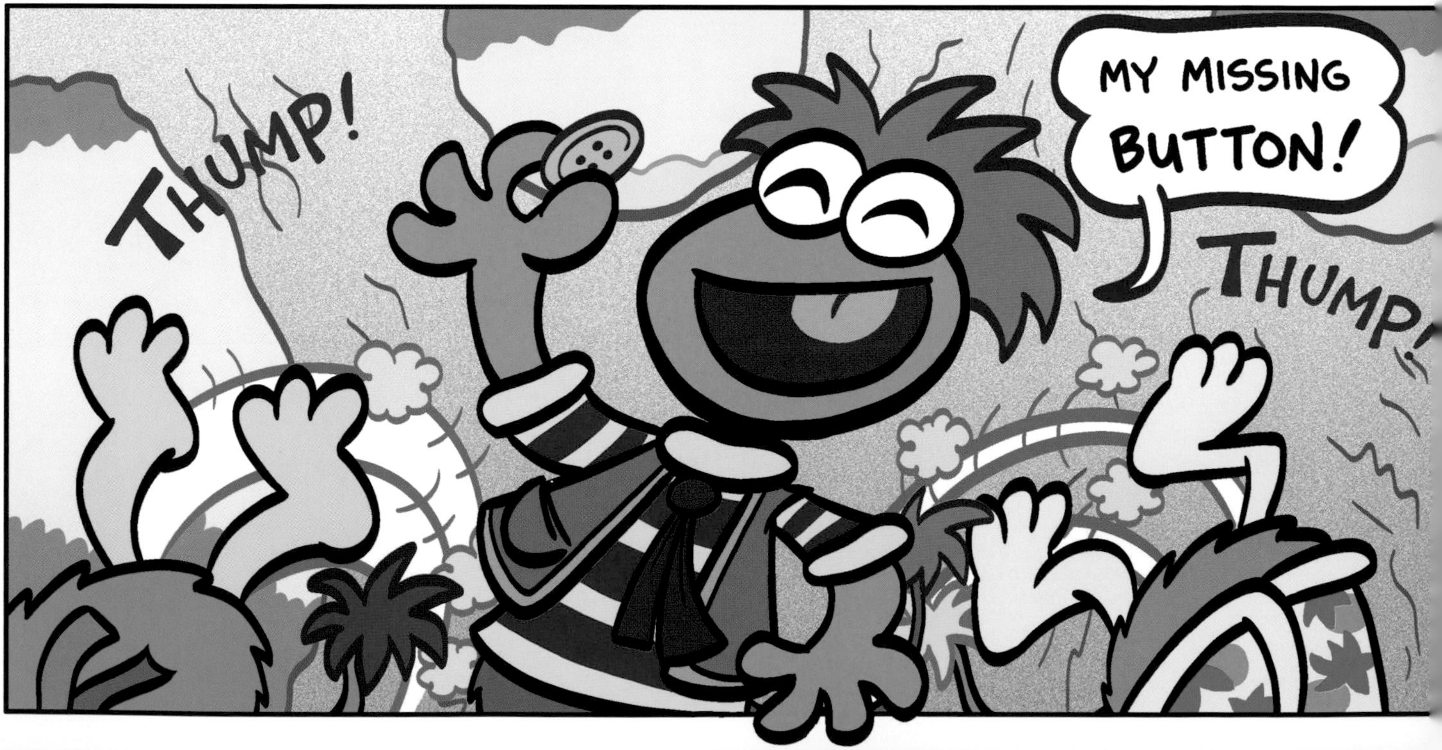
THUMP!
MY MISSING BUTTON!
THUMP!

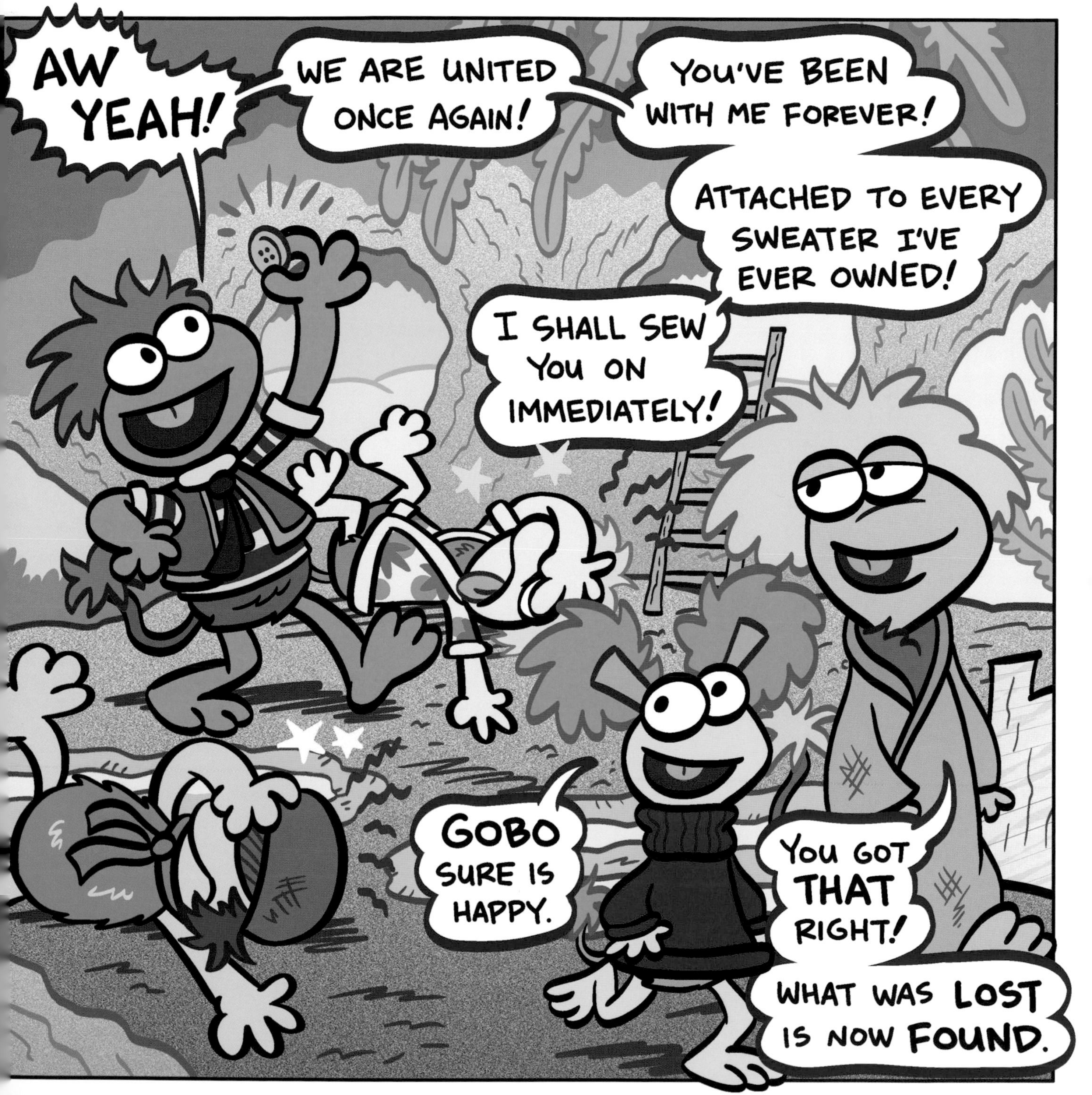
AW YEAH!
WE ARE UNITED ONCE AGAIN!
YOU'VE BEEN WITH ME FOREVER!
ATTACHED TO EVERY SWEATER I'VE EVER OWNED!
I SHALL SEW YOU ON IMMEDIATELY!
GOBO SURE IS HAPPY.
YOU GOT THAT RIGHT!
WHAT WAS LOST IS NOW FOUND.

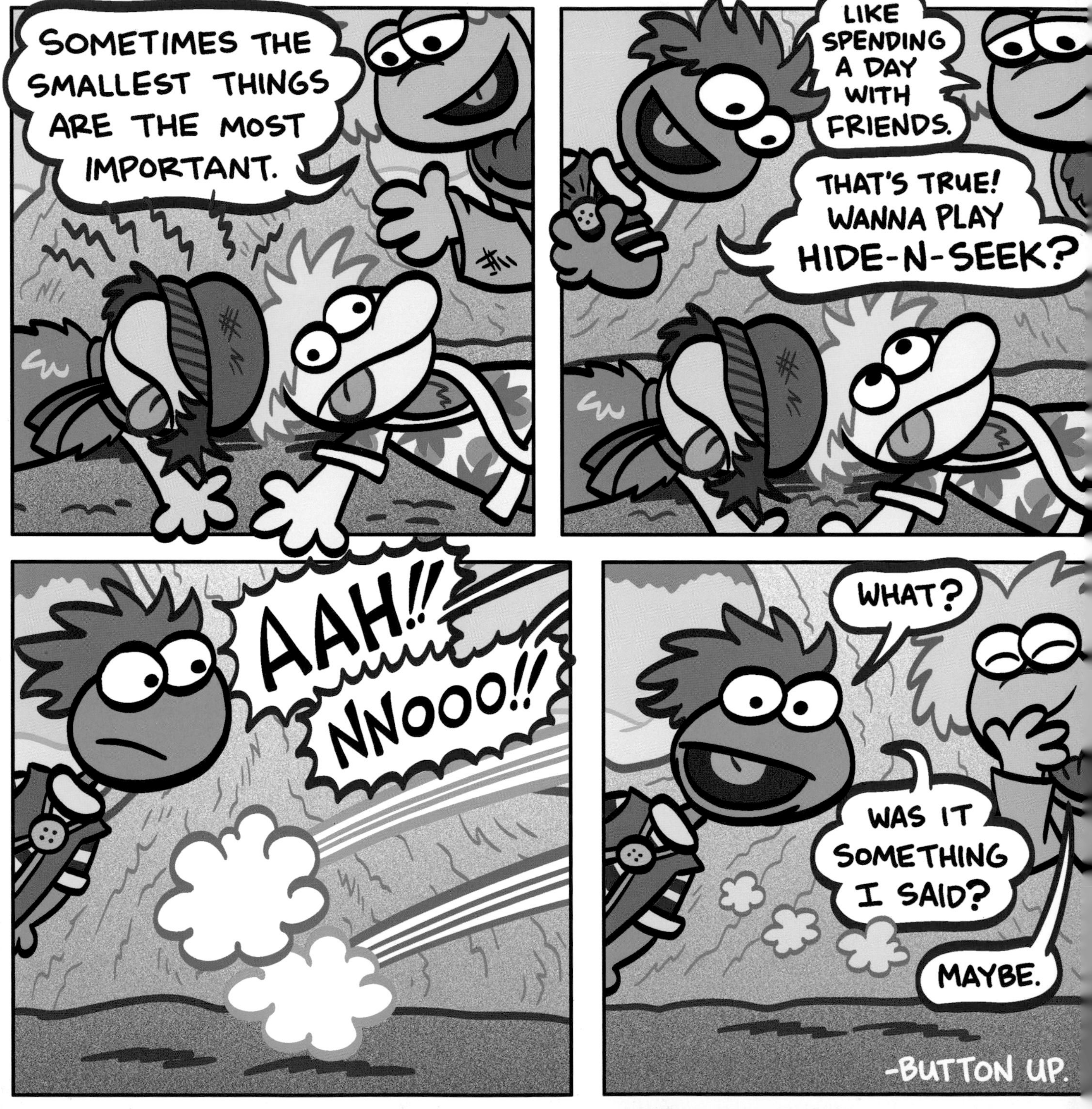
SOMETIMES THE SMALLEST THINGS ARE THE MOST IMPORTANT.
LIKE SPENDING A DAY WITH FRIENDS.
THAT'S TRUE! WANNA PLAY HIDE-N-SEEK?
AAH!!
NNOOO!!
WHAT?
WAS IT SOMETHING I SAID?
MAYBE.
-BUTTON UP.

DISCOVER
THE WORLD OF JIM HENSON

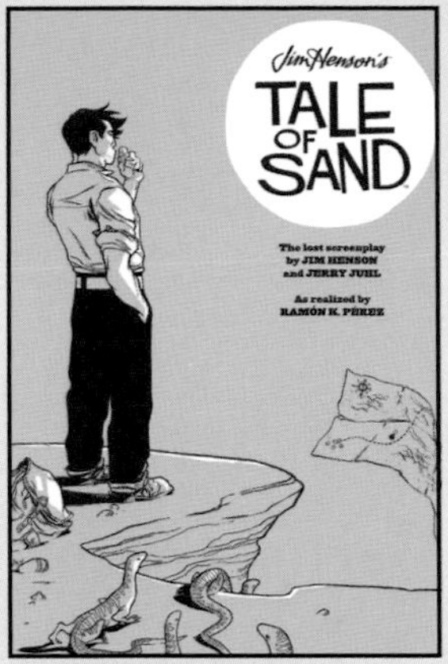
Jim Henson's
TALE OF SAND
The lost screenplay by JIM HENSON and JERRY JUHL
As realized by RAMÓN K. PÉREZ

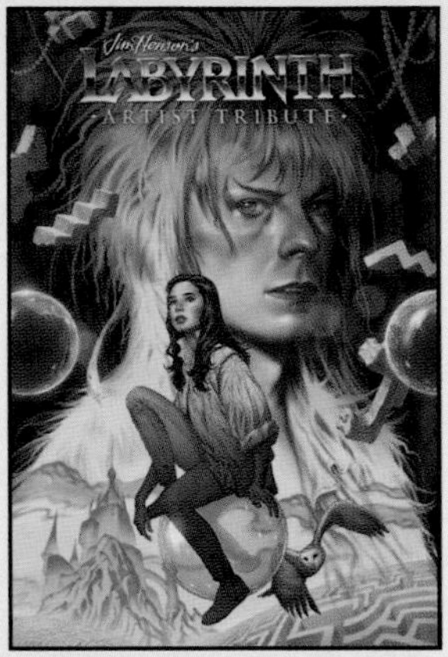
Jim Henson's
LABYRINTH
ARTIST TRIBUTE

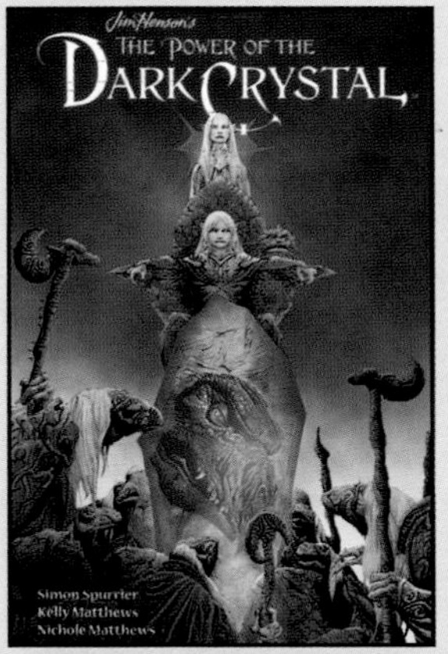
Jim Henson's
THE POWER OF THE
DARK CRYSTAL
Simon Spurrier
Kelly Matthews
Nichole Matthews

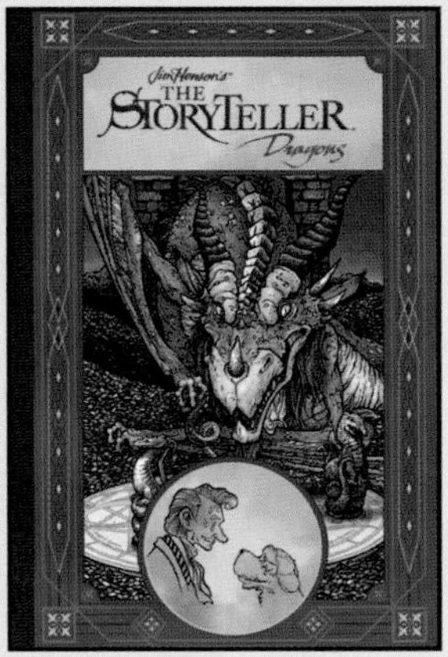
Jim Henson's
THE STORYTELLER
Dragons

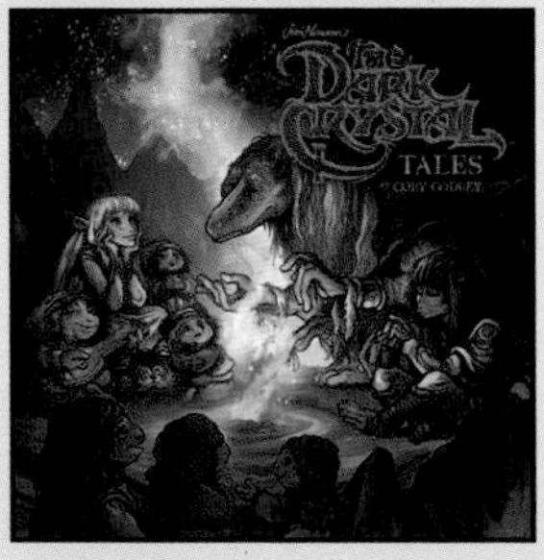
Jim Henson's
The Dark Crystal
TALES

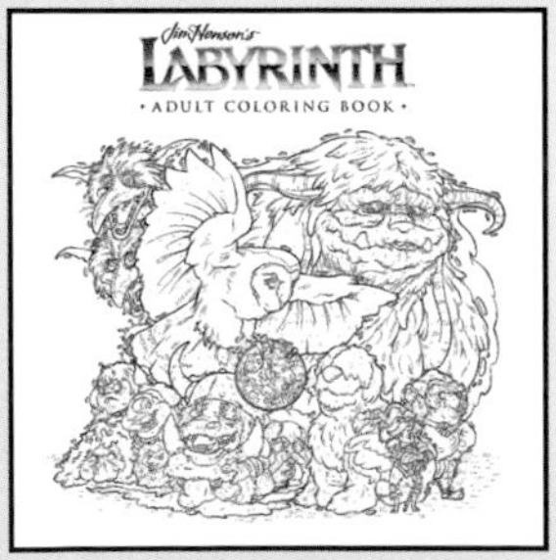
Jim Henson's
LABYRINTH
ADULT COLORING BOOK

ARCHAIA™

AVAILABLE AT YOUR LOCAL COMICS SHOP AND BOOKSTORE

WWW.**BOOM-STUDIOS**.COM

Jim Henson's Tale of Sand
Jim Henson, Jerry Juhl, Ramón K. Pérez
ISBN: 978-1-93639-309-1 | $29.95 US

Jim Henson's The Dark Crystal: Creation Myths
Brian Froud, Alex Sheikman, Joshua Dysart, and others
Volume 1
ISBN: 978-1-60886-704-2 | $14.99 US
Volume 2
ISBN: 978-1-60886-887-2 | $14.99 US
Volume 3
ISBN: 978-1-60886-906-0 | $14.99 US

Jim Henson's The Power of the Dark Crystal
Simon Spurrier, Kelly and Nichole Matthews
Volume 1
ISBN: 978-1-60886-992-3 | $24.99 US

Jim Henson's The Dark Crystal Tales
Cory Godbey
ISBN: 978-1-60886-845-2 | $16.99 US

Jim Henson's Labyrinth Artist Tribute
Michael Allred, Dave McKean, Faith Erin Hicks, and others
ISBN: 978-1-60886-897-1 | $24.99 US

Jim Henson's Labyrinth Adult Coloring Book
Jorge Corona, Jay Fosgitt, Phil Murphy
ISBN: 978-1-68415-111-0 | $16.99 US

Jim's Henson's The Musical Monsters of Turkey Hollow
Jim Henson, Jerry Juhl, Roger Langridge
ISBN: 978-1-60886-434-8 | $24.99 US

Jim Henson's The Storyteller: Witches
S.M. Vidaurri, Kyla Vanderklugt, Matthew Dow Smith, Jeff Stokely
ISBN: 978-1-60886-747-9 | $24.99 US

Jim Henson's The Storyteller: Dragons
Daniel Bayliss, Jorge Corona, Hannah Christensen, Nathan Pride
ISBN: 978-1-60886-874-2 | $24.99 US